OLIVER CRUM AND THE GRIM MENAGERIE

OLIVER CRUM BOOK 2

CHRIS COOPER

DREADFUL
MEDIA

Oliver Crum and the Grim Menagerie

Published by Dreadful Media

Enjoy the book? Please consider leaving a review at goodreads.com or amazon.com. Every review helps. To receive news of new publications, events, and exclusive offers, please sign up for the Dreadful Media Newsletter on our website.
WWW.DREADFULMEDIA.COM

CHAPTER ONE

Fireflies speckled the night air like burning embers. A cabin was nestled between a pair of maple trees, its dilapidated roof bowing as if it were a hammock strung between them. Firelight flickered in the window as Oliver approached cautiously, frosted grass crunching under his feet. When he ducked under the sill, the cabin provided a momentary reprieve from the icy wind cutting through his T-shirt. He wasn't sure what had driven him to wander into the cold wearing nothing but a set of flimsy pajamas, but he was certain the answer lay inside the broken-down building.

Oliver peered through the window, poking his head above the frame just enough to see inside. The cabin was sparsely decorated, although some attempt had been made to repair its rotting walls. The crumbling beams holding up the ceiling joists had been rein-forced with new wood, and several fresh planks left a haphazard pattern in the floor where the bad boards had been replaced. Much like the man inside, the building seemed to be on its last legs.

A leather wingback chair sat perched in front of a roaring fire, so close to the flames that the figure resting in it must have been roasting. At a glance, the shriveled man with desiccated skin appeared to be a corpse, but further inspection revealed the subtle rise and fall of his chest. He pulled a wool blanket farther up his lap and tightly around his waist. The elaborate cane lying next to him was enough to give Simon Hale's identity away, and the sinister glint in his eye hadn't aged away like the rest of his body.

Oliver had hoped the man was long dead. Simon had strolled into the sleepy town of Christchurch a little over a year before from the secret town of Briar-wood, a town hidden in the woods and obscured by an invisible barrier through which only he and those in possession of the Briarwood key could cross. Although Oliver managed to save the town from Simon and his murderous witch of a daughter, the man had left several dead and the rest of Christchurch drowning in fear.

Simon's cough penetrated the single-pane windows of the cabin, and he reached for a wineglass on the table next to him. He brought the glass to his lips, and the deep-red liquid slowly trickled into his mouth. The wine may have coated the back of his throat momentarily, but the cough came again, guttural and from deep within his chest. Simon reached for the glass but accidentally knocked it over, sending it crashing to the floor. Wine seeped through the floorboards as broken glass sparkled in the firelight.

Oliver flashed back to the chamber in the Briarwood town hall, where Simon had stood in front of him, lips soaked with the blood of his own son—blood that could somehow heal wounds and slow the inevitable effects of age on the body.

Without his son's blood to sustain him, time had caught up with Simon Hale, and his body slumped forward and fell to the floor.

Oliver had no reason to help. The man had orchestrated the murder of several people in Christchurch, tortured his subjects in Briarwood, and abused his own children. Death by old age was too kind a punishment, if a punishment at all.

Oliver waited for the man's chest to come to rest and yearned for final assurance that Simon was no longer a threat. As he backed away from the window and into the biting wind, the subtle glow from the fire grew brighter. Simon's blanket must have fallen too close to the flames and caught. Oliver stood and looked inside. The fire had crawled onto the blanket, creeping slowly closer to Simon's body.

It's over. The fire would ensure it. He felt a weight lift from his shoulders and exhaled as if he had been holding his breath for the past year.

The building went up quickly, and soon the scene inside was completely wiped away by flame. He stood close to the cabin at first, warming himself in the radiant heat, but the fire became too hot, and he was forced to step away.

Bursts of ash replaced the flecks of firefly glow as they shot up through a hole in the roof, where the tiles had peeled away and fallen into the inferno below. He backed away to watch the building crumble, although not far enough to leave the protective warmth completely.

Once little remained of the cabin, aside from a charred doorframe and a few foundation timbers, Oliver turned to face the cold, unsure of how he would get home. *Where is home?* He marched forward and stepped outside the ring of soggy earth where the blaze had melted the snow. Trees encircled the clearing, and the only way out was through the snowy forest.

As he reached the tree line, he heard a whoosh of flame sneak up on him, and a wall of fire shot up in front of him, blocking his path. Oliver turned toward the cabin. Simon stood in the charred doorway, skin scorched and peeling from his bones, the metal bits of his cane red-hot and glowing. The man said nothing at first but stood, black eyes tracing Oliver's movements.

"What do you want from me?" Oliver asked.

Simon's scream echoed through the clearing as flames burst from his lips. He stepped down from the cabin and limped toward Oliver, and the ground hissed under his feet.

Oliver wanted to flee, but flames surrounded him. He had no place to go but toward the cabin—toward the man who surely wanted to kill him. His heart pounded as Simon raised his cane, but before the man could press the hot metal tip into Oliver's chest, Oliver turned and leapt through the wall of fire.

Oliver shot up in bed and frantically tried to put out the flames, which had disappeared once he left the dream world. His sweat soaked the covers, and he'd sent his fat tabby, Nekko, flying to the floor. For just a moment, he swore he felt a burning sensation under his shirt.

The nightmares had been frequent this week. Eric, the Christchurch chief of police, had brought news of Simon's death in prison, which stirred up all the raw emotions from last year's events. Some nights, Oliver faced Simon in a flaming cabin, and others, he ran from the Witch—Simon's daughter—who he'd forced to terrorize Oliver's town.

His nightstand alarm clock read four in the morning. He wouldn't need to rise for several more hours but found the prospect of more sleep unlikely.

Izzy and Anna could probably use my help to prep for the flea market anyway.

Nekko looked up at him with indignation as he ripped his sweaty sheets from the bed and threw them into a pile on the floor.

He looked out onto the front yard, where the police cruiser had lain flipped a year before. The townspeople had wiped away the signs of the attack, filling the deep gashes in the earth and planting new grass seed, but the impact on his psyche remained. The story still felt unfinished to him, and perhaps that was why his mind refused to let it go. After all the damage Simon had caused, Oliver found it hard to believe the man had died without so much as a whimper.

Nekko had taken ownership of his pillow since Oliver was out of bed. She circled a few times then lay down, her body sinking into the soft memory foam.

"Guess you deserve it, for the scare I gave you," he said, scratching underneath her chin.

He descended the staircase to the living room. Izzy had used the destruction caused by the Witch's attack last year as an excuse to redecorate. Although she lived firmly in the northeast, she'd become obsessed with southwestern style, adding her own twists, of course.

She'd painted much of the living room furniture turquoise then sanded pieces down to give them a more rustic look. She replaced the rug with a burnt-orange-and-red-zigzag one and lined the shelves with miniature Kokopelli figurines. She loathed the thought of hanging real antlers from her wall, so instead she sculpted artificial ones out of clay.

Izzy sat at the kitchen table, drinking a thick green concoction out of a tall glass.

"Juicing again?" he asked.

"Juicing is out. The pulp is where it's at. Want some?" She tipped her glass in his direction before taking another large gulp. The remainder of the drink clung to the sides of the glass before collecting in a chunky pool at the bottom.

"I'll pass," he replied, pouring himself a cup of coffee.

Izzy shrugged. "You'll be sorry when I outlive you."

Oliver corrected her with a smirk. "I'll be dead, so I won't care."

"What are you doing up this early, anyway? Another nightmare?"

He nodded. "The flaming cabin one this time."

"Valerian—that's what you need."

"What's valerian?"

"An herb. Should help you sleep. I'm growing it along the side of the house. I'll pick some for you."

Oliver sat next to her and picked up a hand-scrawled list on the table. "Think this will be enough? The turnout's supposed to be huge."

"We could double it if you're sure everything will sell."

"Do we have time for that?" he asked.

"Should be able to pull it off before you two need to leave. Let's double it. I trust you," she replied.

Oliver had convinced Izzy to invest in a table at the flea market in Amberley, a town just a short drive from Christchurch. They'd sold baked goods and honey at a few farmers' markets last year when times at the bakery were tough. This flea market would be four or five times the size.

"If the flea goes well, we ought to make it a recurring thing," he said.

"You're my own little Rockefeller," she replied. "Can't decide if I'm proud or disgusted."

"I'm serious. This could be great for the bakery."

"Well, better get to work then. So much to bake, so little time. Want to ride with me?" She swigged the last of her viscous smoothie and stood up.

Oliver nodded and refilled his coffee cup.

Izzy had lamented the death of her old station wagon until she and Oliver painted the new one with caricatures and designs that put those on her old one to shame. She insisted Oliver paint himself and Anna on the hood. They'd even left enough room to add Pan, Izzy's black-and-tan corgi, above the left wheel well.

Christchurch slept as Izzy pulled the car through the street next to the town square, passing the statue Simon had gone careening into just a year before.

Anna had arrived at the bakery an hour earlier to prep the ingredients for the morning's bakes. Izzy had scraped together a few extra bucks an hour and promoted Anna to head baker in the winter when the arthritis in Izzy's hands became so painful that she could barely do more than lift an empty cake tin. Although she would never admit it, Oliver was certain Izzy was slowly removing herself from the bakery's day-to-day operations. As Anna picked up the slack in the kitchen and Oliver became more involved in the bookkeeping, Izzy would fill in as needed, mostly as Anna's unofficial kitchen assistant.

Now that Izzy had made peace with the town Elders, the group of senior rule enforcers who ensured Christchurch residents followed town policy to the letter, they'd come to a mutual understanding about the bakery's exterior. She was free to decorate the front courtyard with as many gnomes, pipe dragons, and obscure topiaries as she wished as long as the building itself was left to look like all the others around it. Izzy still had moments of rebellion, but she chose her battles more wisely.

Anna stood next to one of the large mixers with her back turned toward Oliver and Izzy, a heavy sack of flour slung over her shoulder. She had lined the counters with wicker baskets, and the room already smelled of freshly baked bread.

"About time you rolled out of bed. It's nearly four thirty." She finished emptying the flour sack and turned around. "Oliver! Didn't expect to see you this early. Nightmares again?"

Oliver nodded as Izzy pulled a fresh apron from the drawer next to the sink.

"Well, glad you decided to come. I'm running behind and could use some extra muscle."

He looked around. "And where do you expect to find muscle?" He laughed.

"Load up the baskets while Izzy and I get these cookies going."

By seven o'clock, he had filled Izzy's station wagon to the brim with trays of cookies and baskets of bread and muffins and stacked and strapped several folding tables to the luggage rack.

"Sure you don't want to come with us?" Anna asked.

"Who will run the bakery? Pan?" Izzy replied.

"Not Nekko. She'd eat us out of business," Anna added.

"Next time. You two have fun, and good luck!"

Izzy waved as Oliver backed the station wagon down the driveway and onto the street.

The sun rose over the horizon as they drove past the Christchurch welcome sign and toward the back roads leading to Amberley.

CHAPTER TWO

Leaves rustled on the trees as a late-September breeze blew through the park. The large oaks were still clinging tightly to their leaves although their colors had shifted from green to oranges and yellows, mimicking the shades of a brilliant sunrise.

Amberley was much smaller than the city from which Oliver had escaped the year before, but compared to Christchurch, it was a metropolis. The place was a college town of sorts, with a small arts school up the road that drew in all sorts of eclectic creators.

Soon, the Amberley Flea would be in full swing, and thousands of visitors would descend upon the park and its rows and rows of canvas tents to buy everything from vegetables to artisanal mustache waxes. The town always held the flea market in the first two weeks of fall, when summer had yet to fully release its grip on the city.

Although Amberley lacked the rural charm of Christchurch, it made up for it with a larger supply of paying customers. Izzy wouldn't admit it, but Oliver was fairly certain she'd struggled to pay him with the profits from Christchurch customers alone. He tried to decline his pay a few times, but she wouldn't have it. Fortunately, times had gotten better, but when he'd suggested looking for more events outside town to boost revenue, she had been quick to mention the Amberley Flea.

After unstacking the folding tables from the roof of the station wagon, Oliver and Anna set them in a U shape around the canvas tent. While Anna arranged the jars of honey on the front table, Oliver arranged the large wicker baskets of baked goods. The smell of cinnamon caught his nose as he pulled the plastic wrap off a tray full of pecan rolls.

A steady stream of early birds trickled through the booths, and Anna sold three jars of honey before the flea officially opened.

"If today carries on like this, we'll have to come back next weekend," she said.

"The booth fee was a gamble, but seems like it's going to be worth it," Oliver added. He'd cut a few dowels at the bakery earlier and fashioned them into makeshift pricing signs, which he stuck down into the baskets.

As he reached into one of the baskets to straighten a sign, a hand casually brushed against his, catching him by surprise.

"Sorry, didn't mean to scare you. Mind if I set a few of these on your table?" the woman asked.

The thirtysomething wore a short-sleeved dress with a lace skirt, and deep tattoos lined her arms with intricate latticework. Her frizzy hair, along with the rest of her attire, was jet-black and looked as if she'd taken a long convertible ride with the top down. Winged eyeliner poked out from behind a pair of large round sunglasses. She stood gripping a handful of flyers.

"Sure, go ahead," he replied, cracking a courteous smile.

She slid several of the flyers underneath the corner of a basket of blueberry muffins. "I'm Ruby, by the way. Pleased to meet you." She extended her hand.

"Oliver," he replied. "And this is Anna."

"Nice to meet you," Anna popped up over Oliver's shoulder.

"The show starts at eight, and it's our opening night," Ruby said. "You should stop by if you have the chance. We're right by the church."

"Hopefully, we can make it," Oliver replied.

"And I'll be doing readings all day and would love to read you," she added, pointing at the booth between the Peter's Pickles and bubble-tea booths. Ruby had covered its ugly striped canvas with violet fabric and transformed the tent into a cozy bohemian den of sorts. A circular table sat atop a red patterned rug, and she had lined the makeshift room's borders with pillows.

"Think we need to step up our decorating game. Your booth puts ours to shame," he said.

"Thank you. It's even nicer when you're inside. Hope to see you later." With a sly smile and a nod, Ruby was on her way to the next booth, the heels of her long leather boots sinking into the semisoft earth.

"Well, someone's made a new friend," Anna said from behind.

"What do you mean?"

"She was flirting with you." She straightened a basket of baguettes on the back table. "You should stop by her booth."

"Sure she's just trying to drum up business." He watched Ruby float across the aisle to Peter's Pickles and approach whom he assumed was Peter. "See?"

"Have some confidence."

"If she's flirting, she's currently flirting with a middle-aged man who's somehow converted his comb-over into a ponytail and has clearly eaten an unhealthy amount of his own product. She's not exactly my type, anyway."

"Oh, you have a type? I assumed you were asexual."

"I am not asexual," he replied defensively.

"What's your type then? Tall, blonde, and skinny?"

Oliver searched for a way to change the subject and picked up a flyer. "Mistress Ruby's Grim Menagerie. Sounds weird, don't you think?"

"You're not getting off that—" Anna peered over his shoulder at the poster. "What kind of show is this?" The front of the flyer was black with a skeletal bat spreading its wings across the page. "What's a menagerie?"

"No idea. From the looks of the flyer, a dead-bat puppet show. Might be fun," he joked.

"Always wanted to see a dead-bat puppet show," she replied.

By the end of the day, they'd sold off most of their honey supply, and the baked goods had dwindled to a few baskets of odds and ends. The other merchants packed up their tents, so Anna and Oliver followed suit.

Oliver pitched the Grim Menagerie flyers into the trash bin as he cleared off the folding tables.

"So that's a no on the show then?" Anna asked.

"Unfortunately, Nekko and I have already made

firm arrangements. I'm going to sit on the couch and sketch while she walks back and forth across my lap and tries to lie on the sketch pad."

"Well, wouldn't want to disrupt such a fun evening."

"You're welcome to join although I don't think I have a pad large enough for you to walk across."

"I'll pass—thank you very much."

Once they loaded everything into the car and affixed the tables firmly to the roof, they made the short drive back to Christchurch. After unloading at the bakery, Oliver drove Anna back to her cottage then returned home.

He'd thought about trying to find a place of his own, but his bakery salary made that a challenge. Christchurch wasn't exactly full of affordable housing. He also enjoyed having a human to come home to. Nekko provided a great deal of companionship but was terrible at holding conversations. Izzy kept him on his toes and ensured he didn't spend too much time inside his own head. Although she was his great aunt, their relationship was more friendly than familial.

The sky darkened as the last sliver of sunlight vanished over the horizon, but all the lights in the front of Izzy's house were off. Pan greeted him as he unlocked the door, but Izzy was nowhere in sight. He walked through the dark living room and toward a dim light coming from the kitchen, nearly tripping over Izzy's handmade Native American drum on the journey.

She was sitting at the kitchen table, the room lit only by a small nightlight plugged into the counter outlet. She took a swig from a bottle of Irish cream when she noticed Oliver.

"Are you drinking straight cream? Had a rough evening, I'm guessing?" he asked.

"It's the hardest stuff I could find." Izzy avoided eye contact. "I messed up big time, kiddo."

Oliver pulled up a chair on the other side of the table and sat across from her. "Surely nothing bad enough for this dramatic response."

She took another swig from the bottle. "I told your mom you've been staying with me."

"What?" He felt the color drain from his face.

"She knows you lost your job in the city and have been helping me with the bakery."

Oliver reached for the bottle and took a giant gulp. The mix of whiskey and cream was sickly. "Why would you tell her?"

"She pressed me. You know I don't hold up well under interrogation," Izzy replied.

"Why would she even think to call you?"

"Apparently, she tried to send you a package, and it came back as an incorrect address."

"But I had my mail forwarded."

"Well, they must have crossed wires somewhere. She knows, and there's no going back now."

Oliver had been careful to hide his move from his mother. He typically avoided confrontation at all costs, and Bev Crum was a walking, talking confrontation. He'd worked hard for his mother's approval, which had played a large part in him taking a job in the city, and he knew how disappointed she would be if she found out he traded his suit in for an apron. Fortunately, she didn't have caller ID, and they rarely spoke, so the task hadn't been that difficult. He had planned on telling her, but the longer he waited, the more difficult it had become.

"How am I going to explain that I've been lying to her for an entire year?"

"Don't you think it's time to come clean? You're twenty-five, and you're still scared of your mom." The whiskey had made Izzy feisty.

"Aren't *you* still scared of her? Isn't that why you rolled over on me?" he shot back.

"I think you're missing the point," she said defensively. "Don't you want her to know about your life? Surely, she'll be happy for you when she sees how well you're doing here."

"Want to bet? She'll end up trying to convince me to leave—just watch. And she'll do it while slipping in a ton of passive-aggressive comments about the way we live."

"Your mom has her hang-ups, but she cares about you. She wants to make sure you're doing all right."

"No, she wants to make sure I'm not embarrassing the family. I assume she'll want me to call and explain?"

"No need," Izzy replied.

"Why not? Is she so angry she doesn't want to talk?"

"She'll be on the afternoon train on Friday. You'll have the privilege of explaining in person."

The sensation in Oliver's stomach was reminiscent of when the Briarwood Witch had lifted him up by his insides.

She took another swig from the bottle. "Your mom's coming to Christchurch."

After commiserating and finishing nearly half the bottle of Irish cream, Izzy and Oliver turned in for the evening. Nekko grew annoyed by Oliver's constant tossing and turning and moved to the windowsill to watch the yard below.

No matter how hard he tried, Oliver couldn't rid his mind of his mother's impending visit. He felt guilty for keeping such a large change in his life from her, but he'd known how she would react. He hated disappointing her—always had—but he felt childish for refusing to stand up for himself. She would be angry for sure, but telling the truth would have saved him a lot of mental anguish. He wasn't sure why she had always made him so nervous. Perhaps her need to criticize was the perfect foil for his need to please.

After several hours of restlessness, Oliver slipped into a paranoid sleep, just in time for the sun to rise.

CHAPTER THREE

On the day of the big visit, Oliver spent the morning filling orders between waiting tables at the bakery. Once the lunch rush died down, he and Izzy set off to pick his mother up from the train station, leaving Anna to prep the bakery for the morning.

Izzy spotted Martin waving from across the square. "Let's stop over and say hello before we go to the station." She, too, must have been trying to prolong their walk as much as possible and seemed to sense Oliver's uneasiness.

Martin was touching up the woodwork on the bay window at the front of Fletcher Antiquities, and maroon paint speckled his forest-green sweater.

"Brush get away from you, Martin?" Izzy asked.

"Fortunately, this isn't my good sweater." He smirked. "Glad I caught you. Stumbled upon a chimney pot at an estate sale this weekend. I've got it in the back of the shop, if you want to take a look."

Izzy's face lit up. "You finally found a spare one!" She looked at her watch, and her smile faded. "I'll have to come back another time, though. Oliver's mom is in for the week, and her train arrives in a minute or two."

"No worries," Martin replied. "I'll keep it aside for you. Your mom's in town, eh, Oliver? Bring her by the shop. I'd love to meet her."

"Will do." Oliver grimaced. As they turned toward the station, he looked at Izzy. "Chimney pot?"

"Oh, I'm sure you'd know one if you saw it. It's a clay column that sits—" She spun around and pointed at the top of the antique shop. "See the clay thing on top of the brick chimney? That's a chimney pot. I need one for a new fountain design, but they're expensive and hard to find. Martin promised to hunt one down for me."

They passed under the archway to Christchurch station, just in time to see the arriving train squeal to a halt.

Oliver felt himself clamming up as Izzy stepped toward the edge of the platform.

"Relax," she said, giving him a side-eye.

At first, he couldn't find his mother. *Maybe she missed the train.* His hopes were dashed when he saw her bleached-blond pixie cut slowly bobbing down the aisle.

"There she is," he said.

They camped out under the lamppost nearest to her exit. When the sliding door opened, Beverly Crum stepped out, tugging a piece of leather luggage behind her. Although the train ride must have been several hours long, her coral slacks and cream-colored blazer were still perfectly pressed and wrinkle free. She said nothing when she saw Oliver at first, just stood for a moment, scowling. Just as Oliver thought he was going to be sick, as if someone hit a reset switch on the back of her neck, his mother's scowl rose to a wide grin.

"Well, give your mother a hug." She opened her arms. She was a good foot shorter than Oliver—he'd gotten his height from his father's side of the family—but she had the grip of a grizzly bear. She pulled back but held firmly to his waist. "Your hair's all mussed." She used a hand to fix his cowlick that had been blown out of place by the breeze. "You've let it grow so long!"

"It's fine." Oliver pulled away and ran his fingers through his hair.

She turned toward Izzy. "Isabelle, so good to see you. I see you're still as fashionable as ever." She went in for another awkward hug.

Izzy wore a pair of denim overalls, which she'd draped with a bright floral shawl. Oliver had seen some of Izzy's more interesting outfits over the last year, and this was conservative in comparison.

"Always a pleasure, Bev," Izzy replied. "If you're ready, I thought we'd stop by the bakery on the way home so you can have a look around."

"We're walking, then?" she asked. "I had a hunch. Let me slip on more comfortable shoes." Bev sat on a station bench and swapped her heels out for a pair of gym shoes.

"You wore heels on the train?" Izzy asked. "Why not flats?"

"Comfort is never an excuse to look like a slouch. Never know who you might run into. Station wagon having issues again?"

"No, no. Just thought it would be nice to walk," Izzy replied.

"Let's be off," Bev said, hopping up from the bench. "Lead the way."

Izzy guided the pack through the station and toward the bakery. Anna had already locked up for the afternoon when she finished in the kitchen, but Izzy pulled a ring of keys from her pocket and unlocked the front door.

"Bev, meet the bakery," Izzy said.

Bev walked along the U-shaped counter and admired the artwork on the walls. "It's so quaint. You manage all of this by yourself?"

"Oliver's taken on quite a few responsibilities, and one of our friends from town works here too," Izzy replied, ignoring the subtle jab.

"Good to see you've finally outgrown your starving-artist phase."

"Oh, you sound just like your mother. Art is still a large part of my life." Izzy gestured around the room. "You know, your son has a penchant for paint too." She pointed at the mural on the far wall. "He's got some interesting ideas for Halloween."

Bev stepped over to the mural on the other side of the bakery. The piece featured caricatures of many of the bigger town personalities. Oliver had painted it the previous summer and had been adding to it ever since. Unlike the more controversial works in Izzy's studio, this one was a friendly gesture for the townspeople, and it was a hit. Even Madeline, the leader of the town Elders, found the images amusing, and Madeline rarely found anything amusing.

"I didn't know you still liked to doodle," Bev said. "Thought you stopped a long time ago."

"I've picked it up again. Izzy's been a great inspiration," he replied.

Anna cleared her throat from behind the counter. "Isn't anyone going to introduce me?"

"Mom, this is Anna. Anna, this is my mom, Bev."

"A pleasure to meet you, Anna," Bev replied. "My,

you are a pretty one, aren't you?" She turned her head and gave Oliver a sly smile.

"Um, thanks," she replied. She shot Oliver a puzzled look.

He turned to Bev. "She's not my girlfriend."

"Oh no, definitely not." Anna laughed hard enough to make Oliver feel self-conscious.

"Shame," Bev replied.

"Let's head to the house." Oliver tried to steer the conversation away from his nonexistent love life. "I'm sure you're exhausted from the ride."

"I could use a breather and a glass of wine," Bev replied.

"To the wine, then!" Izzy raised her fist.

Bev huffed and puffed all the way to Izzy's house while Oliver wheeled her heavy suitcase behind him. Although she'd made a few remarks, her demeanor pleasantly surprised him. She had to be upset with him, but she wasn't showing it outwardly. Perhaps she had changed since they'd last seen each other. He'd changed, so it was only reasonable to assume she'd done the same.

Pan heard the trio approaching and barked frantically at the other side of the door, little paws clawing at the wood.

"Never imagined you as the yappy-dog type, Isabelle," Bev said.

"Pan is not *yappy*," Izzy shot back as if Bev had just insulted her child.

His mother shooed Pan away with her foot, but a simple tennis shoe to the face wasn't enough to deter the resilient corgi.

"Pet him, or he won't leave you alone," Oliver said.

She made one last attempt to sweep the pup away with her foot before relenting. She leaned over and gave Pan three staccato pats on the head. "All right, now go bother someone else."

Pan sat on his haunches and stared.

"Go on," she added, flicking her wrist.

Pan refused to move. Izzy shook the treat bag in the kitchen, and he scampered off into the other room.

"Think you've made a new friend," Oliver said.

"I have enough friends already," Bev replied. "Oh my—is that Nekko?" She pointed at the butterscotch whale perched on the windowsill.

Nekko turned her head toward them, momentarily pulled away from the squirrels playing on the lawn outside.

"That's her. Think she's been bulking up so Pan doesn't have a weight advantage over her," he replied.

"She's so fat!"

Nekko turned her head at the insult. Her fat rolls hung over the edge of the windowsill like a cellulite curtain.

"We keep her on a strict diet. She's just lazy and has bad kitty genes," Oliver said defensively.

"It's not work—" Bev caught herself midsentence and changed the subject. "Help me with my suitcase, will you?"

Oliver lugged the leather suitcase up the stairs to the guest bedroom on the third floor and set it on the bed. For the first time since his childhood, his mother would be right across the hall from him. Bev might have been a homemaker for most of her life, but she doubled as an amateur sleuth. He had tried to stay up late as a kid, plugging his headphones into the bedroom TV, but she could always hear the chatter from across the hall. She had a nose for lies, and sneaking anything by the woman was impossible, especially when she slept ten feet away.

"So many stairs," Bev said. "Looks like I'll be getting a good workout while I'm here."

"Izzy's setting dinner out on the back porch. I'll let you get unpacked, but come join us once you're done."

"Will do," she replied, unzipping her suitcase.

Oliver turned to leave but stopped short of the doorway. "I'm glad you're here." The words left his lips before he could stop them, somewhat catching him by surprise.

She turned to him and opened her mouth to speak but hesitated. "I'll be down in a minute," she said.

His mother had said nothing about Oliver's job or decision to move to Christchurch, but he knew it was coming—it had to be.

As the sun sank over the tree line, Izzy whipped up a quick dinner salad and opened a bottle of wine.

His mother waddled down the staircase as Oliver pulled a stack of dishes from the cupboard.

"Izzy climbs those things every day? I may end up sleeping on the couch."

Oliver laughed. "Give me a hand with these, would you?" He nodded toward a set of wineglasses.

"What a beautiful night, don't you think?" Izzy asked as Oliver and his mom brought the dishes outside. She poured glasses of wine while Oliver plated the salad.

"How was the ride in?" Oliver asked.

"Wasn't bad at all," Bev replied. "Met a nice man on the train, and we talked nearly the entire trip. He's headed up to Kingston for some convention."

"Really?" Izzy asked. "Get his number?"

Bev choked on her Chablis.

"What? It's a reasonable question," Izzy added. "Haven't you been seeing anyone lately?"

"No, too soon. It hasn't been *that* long since Glen passed away." Bev ran her thumb along her wedding ring and twirled the diamond around to its proper place.

"It's been five years, Mom. I'd say that's long enough. You ought to think about it," Oliver said.

Bev still held strong to her wedding vows, except for the "til death do us part" bit. As far as Oliver knew, she had dated no one since his father's passing after a massive heart attack while Oliver was away at college.

With his father gone, Bev needed someone else to critique, and Oliver became her pet project, or at least that's how he felt.

"What about you?" Bev asked. "Any girls in your life?"

"Well there is Nekko." He laughed. He and Anna had become great friends, but friends were all they were meant to be, and he was fine with that, despite the consistent prodding from others.

"I'm serious. You're well on your way to thirty, and the longer you wait, the harder it gets."

"Are you telling me I'm hopeless then, Bev?" Izzy took a swig of wine. "I like to think I'm at the peak of my sexual prowess."

Oliver tried to picture Izzy dating, but the thought made him chuckle. She was far too independent to be in a relationship, at least with anyone from Christchurch.

"You've always told me you were married to your art," he said.

"And we've had a wonderful marriage," she added.

Once they had finished eating and Oliver cleared the dishes, Izzy brought out another bottle of wine. "My studio is calling, but I think you two have a lot of catching up to do." She winked at Oliver as she refilled his wineglass and set the bottle on the table.

He shot her a desperate glance, but she was gone before he had a chance to make a verbal plea.

Oliver and his mom sat in silence as he searched for something to talk about.

They started with small talk. Oliver asked about his mother's life back home, and she filled him in on her new role as a board member for a local orchestra. She droned on about her responsibilities and the importance of the position, but it was difficult for him to stay focused on the conversation.

You're an adult—just say something. The thought looped in Oliver's mind until he had mustered up the courage to bring up the topic they'd been avoiding for nearly twenty minutes.

"I'm sorry I didn't tell you," he blurted.

She pounced. "And why the hell didn't you?" Her polite smile faded. She had been waiting for the moment.

"Um, I—"

"Have I not always been there for you? What did I do to deserve to be lied to?"

"I didn't mean to lie to you. It's just—"

"The thought of you working in a bakery and living with Isabelle... How absurd. I'm surprised the woman hasn't already driven the place to financial ruin." She sat back in her chair, put her fingers to her lips, and stared off into the distance.

"Is this what you came here for? To insult one of the few people who has supported me through this whole change?" The dig on Izzy made him angry. Oliver knew the woman had her flaws, but she'd taken him in without so much as a second thought, at least that he could tell.

"Supported you? How could I have supported you if you never bothered to tell me? Here I am, thinking you're making a name for yourself in the city, and you're out here, goofing off."

"Why did you come here, Mom?"

"I came here to stop you from throwing your life in the garbage. We worked so hard to give you opportunities we never had, and I can't just let you squander them." She looked down at her lap and teared up. "What would your father think?"

This struck a nerve, and Oliver's face became white-hot. He sat for a moment, trying to collect himself and prevent her from seeing she'd shaken him. Without saying another word, he poured another glass of wine, stood up, and left his mom sitting on the back porch.

As he climbed the stairs to his room, he heard the scraping of canvas coming from Izzy's studio.

He tried to tiptoe to the third-floor stairs, but he couldn't escape the creak of the old floorboards.

"That was quick," Izzy said from the studio.

He stuck his head through the crack in the door. She stood over a large canvas and squeezed out a blob of red paint from a tube. A blur of colors covered her feet, and it looked as if she'd been using her toes for brushes.

Pan sat in the far corner of the room, tucked away in a tiny doggie bed under a shelf of paint brushes, watching the odd scene unfold.

"What's wrong?" she asked.

Oliver couldn't hide his bright-red face, and Izzy must have picked up on his nervous energy.

"Do you really have to ask?" He took a large swig of wine.

Izzy shrugged her shoulders. "Bev?"

"She's been playing nice, but she unloaded as soon as I apologized for hiding the move from her. She asked me what my father would think about me living with you and working at a bakery and tried to guilt-trip me about not telling her."

"Yikes." She made a long stroke with her big toe. "Well, you left the city a year ago, and the only reason she knows about it is because of me. Think that might give her the right to be a little irritated?"

She shuffled the drop cloth across the room with her feet until she was within arm's length of him.

"Has she ever stopped to consider why I might have kept it from her? I'd never hear the end of how disappointing I was. How do you think it feels to hear you would have disappointed your dead father? To hear you've wasted thousands and thousands of your parents' dollars by not using an education they helped pay for? Can you imagine the stress of having to deal with that? And to have to choose between disappointing your parents and making yourself happy?"

Izzy laughed. "Do you think it thrilled your great grandparents when I spent the year after high school living in a yurt on a communal farm? And look at me now!" Izzy gestured at her paint-covered feet. She had pulled her frizzy gray hair back into a chaotic bun that was splashed with acrylic.

Oliver tried to hold in his laugh.

"Think it made them happy I never married and had kids, when your grandmother married right after high school? Life's tough, kiddo. You will only make it worse if you keep hiding from her. If you don't explain yourself, she has no choice but to jump to her own conclusions."

Izzy's words caught him in the throat.

"You're an adult," she added. "If she doesn't like the truth, then so be it, but you're too old to be sneaking around like a teenager."

Oliver looked down at Izzy's paint-covered feet. "You're right. I should have stood up for myself, told her the truth, and stopped being a baby a long time ago."

Oliver stood over the work in progress. He took a moment to realize what Izzy had painted—an abstract landscape.

He stood and watched her paint for a few minutes until he heard his mom climb the stairs to her bedroom. He waited for her to settle in and lie down, making the box spring squeak. He swallowed his fear and stepped into the hallway.

"Thanks," he said as he took the first step.

"I should charge for these pearls of wisdom," she replied.

He took the stairs to the third floor. The lamplight from Bev's bedroom cast a dim glow across the hardwood floor. He caught himself holding his breath as he approached, and his knock was timid.

"Come in," she said.

Oliver pushed the door open. His mom lay in bed, glasses pushed far down her nose, attempting to focus on the text of her Danielle Steel, which she held out as far as her arms could manage.

He sat on the edge of her bed, a gesture that seemed to catch her off guard. "Can we talk?"

"What can I do for you?" she asked, refusing to look up from her book.

"I shouldn't have stomped off like that. I'm not a child, but the way you talk about Izzy is insulting. She has been nothing but supportive." He rested his hand on her leg.

Bev set her novel facedown on the bed. "Perhaps I was harsh, but you can't blame me for being angry, when you've been lying for an entire year."

"I'm sorry I didn't tell you about the job. I thought I'd take some time off, find another job, and be on my way. I never expected to stay. It all happened so fast, and I didn't want to disappoint you."

"Would you have ever owned up to any of this if I hadn't caught you?" she asked.

Oliver felt the lie on the tip of his tongue but pulled it back. "I would have had to, eventually. I couldn't keep this from you forever, but the longer I waited, the harder it got."

"I see." She looked down at the bed.

"Come with us to the bakery tomorrow morning." He threw out a life preserver. "We're headed over to the flea market in Amberley. You could come with us— see what it's like. We nearly sold out last weekend. I've been managing Izzy's books, too, and business is booming. I think you'd be proud of me if you saw everything in action. It's more work than you think."

"We'll see," she replied.

"All right. Well, at least promise to think about it. We'll be up bright and early. We could make a whole day of it, maybe see the city after the flea market."

She nodded.

"I'll leave you alone now. Maybe we can talk again tomorrow. Have a good night," he said, turning toward the door.

Silence.

Oliver crossed the hall to his bedroom and set his alarm for early morning. Nekko had taken up her typical half of the bed, and he lay down, wide awake and stroking her orange fur.

I did my best, he thought. *The ball's in her court.*

CHAPTER FOUR

Oliver cupped his hands around his coffee mug and let the smell of hazelnut fill his nose.

"She coming?" Izzy asked, pulling a jar of granola from the cupboard.

Oliver shrugged. "I'm sure she heard my alarm, but I think she's still asleep."

"Go wake her up."

"I don't want to bug her. She never said she would go. I'd just hoped..."

Izzy poured a bowl of granola and joined Oliver at the table.

"Juicing not doing it for you anymore?" he asked.

"Needed something crunchy."

Oliver looked at his watch. "Better be off soon to help Anna."

Based on last week's success at the flea market,

they'd planned ahead and had done most of the prep the day before.

Oliver grew impatient, and after several minutes of watching Izzy pick through her bowl for the best bits of dried fruits and nuts, he stood up and headed toward the staircase in the living room.

I will wake her up, he resolved.

As soon as his foot hit the first step, he heard the creak of his mother's door. His spirits lifted as she plodded down the stairs.

"I'm not late, am I?" she asked.

"You're just in time. I was on my way up to get you."

"Shall we head off? I assume I'll be able to grab a bite at the bakery."

Bev entered the kitchen with Oliver following closely behind.

Izzy looked up from her bowl. "Decided to join us for an early morning bake-off?"

"I thought I might as well try it. Has anyone seen my purse?"

"It's by the front door, I believe," Izzy replied. "Go grab it, and we'll meet you out front."

After Bev left the room, Izzy stood up and approached Oliver, resting her hands on his shoulders. "See? Looks like honesty did wonders. For what it's worth, I'm proud of you. Pan's proud of you, too, aren't you Pan?"

Pan popped his head out from underneath the table.

Thunder echoed through the town as they climbed into the station wagon and drove to the bakery. Oliver pulled the car as close as he could to the back door, just in case the rain came early.

Bev helped Oliver fill up the baskets while Anna and Izzy worked the ovens. By midmorning, they'd loaded the station wagon once more and were prepared for the trip to Amberley.

"Coming with us?" Oliver asked Bev as she dabbed her forehead with a kitchen towel.

"I had no idea running a bakery was so much work." She huffed. "I may have to sit this one out. I'm not sure I would be of much use at this point."

"She can stay with me and mind the store." Izzy turned to Bev. "Don't worry, the bakery is always slow on rainy days. I have a few orders to fill, but other than that, we can sit and catch up."

As Anna waited in the car and Oliver grabbed a few last-minute items for the tent, Bev cornered him in the kitchen. "Thanks for the invitation. Glad I came." She opened her arms wide for a hug.

"Me too," he replied, somewhat taken aback by the gesture.

He looked back as he closed the kitchen door behind him, and his mother stood watching with a smile.

"Hopefully, the rain holds off for the market," Anna said as Oliver climbed into the car.

"Mm-hmm," Oliver replied.

"Would be a shame if we couldn't turn a profit today."

"Yup." Oliver kept his eyes locked on the road as he pulled out of town.

"We could always rob a bank on the way back—perhaps knock over a gas station."

"Sounds like a plan."

Anna punched Oliver in the leg. "Hey!"

"What did you do that for?" He tried to massage out the pain.

"What is going on with you?"

"Sorry. I'm shocked that Mom came to the bakery this morning. I didn't expect her to, and it means a lot that she made it."

"I've only met her twice, but she seems fine. Maybe she's a little snooty, but it's clear she cares a lot about you."

"You're right. She's trying, at least."

Anna looked up at the menacing storm clouds. "I really hope this rain holds off."

"The organizers said the rain was supposed to be

spotty. Hopefully, we'll get lucky. It's the last flea of the season, so we should have a good turnout if the weather holds."

The rain started when Oliver and Anna began unloading the station wagon and halted once they'd finished and were under the safe cover of the canvas tent. The clouds cleared by late morning, and a large crowd seemed to follow the sun as people shuffled into the park.

Morning bled into afternoon, and they had little time to rest amidst the flurry of customers. They'd sold most of their baked goods by late afternoon and finally had some downtime.

Oliver looked across the aisle at where Ruby's tent had been. Instead of cozy purple curtains, the new occupant had lined the booth with old mirrors and trays of brass doorknobs. An elderly man sat guard in a folding lawn chair, chewing on a mystery substance like a grazing cow.

"Give me a hand with this, would you?" Anna was trying to lift a large cardboard box of honey onto the table. "He wants a case!"

Oliver turned toward a man who had pulled a large wad of cash from his wallet.

"I was telling Anna here, I bought a jar last week and loved the stuff. I'd like to test it out in my café. If it sells, perhaps we could make some sort of arrangement to carry it regularly."

"Great!" Oliver replied, helping Anna lift the box and place it on the man's cart.

"Izzy will be thrilled," Anna said. "We're completely sold out."

Oliver held up a bun he'd accidentally crushed with his elbow earlier that morning. "What about this guy?"

"A gift for the birds," she replied. "Let's pack up."

"Why don't we go out and have a little fun tonight? The evening's still young. How about a drink after we load up?" Oliver asked. "Might as well see a bit of the city."

"Sounds good. Based on how much money we've made today, we should set up shop here permanently." Anna counted the contents of the money box under the table so as not to draw attention to the large stacks of cash.

"We'll have to keep an eye out for storefronts to rent," she said.

"Can you imagine Izzy running two bakeries?" Oliver asked.

"Good point, and she has a very strong stance against franchises." Anna laughed.

"Still, if people will stock her honey, maybe we

could get Rolling Pin pastries into Amberley shops too."

Once they'd packed everything safely away in the station wagon, the duo walked through the parking lot toward the center of town. Brick row houses and storefronts crammed the Amberley blocks, and music drifted down the narrow streets. They passed an art gallery, which displayed a colorful abstract oil painting in the window.

"Has Izzy ever been here?" Oliver asked. "This place seems much more her style than Christchurch."

"I think she gets her art supplies from a shop next to the college up the road. The rent around here is insane, though. Plus, I think she enjoys playing the role of the town eccentric. She wouldn't be able to do that here. Could you imagine Izzy blending in? She'd be bored to death within a week."

An acoustic crooner belted "The Times They Are a-Changin'" from his perch on the edge of a stone fountain. Anna and Oliver stood on the periphery of a small crowd gathered around the singer.

"Makes me wish I'd gone to college," Anna said. "Spending nights out like this with cool friends, fancy cocktails, and music. What was it like?"

"I wouldn't know," he replied.

Oliver felt out of place—even old—next to the cluster of sharply dressed art students. His college experience had been nothing like this since he'd spent most of his time hunkered in windowless computer labs, poring over textbooks and computer models.

They stood and listened for a moment until Anna spotted a restaurant across the street.

"How about that place?" she asked.

The front window of the storefront held a row of colorful pizzas sitting under a flickering neon sign.

"Pizza?" Oliver asked.

"And Bourbon Bar. Read the sign."

Oliver shrugged and threw a buck into the singer's open guitar case.

The shop was unassuming—just two flour-coated men, two large pizza ovens, and a few empty high-topped tables.

"What can I get for you?" one man asked while the other slipped a pie into the large pizza oven.

"Bourbon, please," Anna replied without hesitation.

The man sighed. "Take the stairs next to the bathroom." He pointed toward the far end of the room.

Anna thanked the man behind the counter, and she walked with Oliver toward the staircase. "Ooh, a speakeasy. How exciting."

As they climbed the steps and rounded the corner, a social buzz filled the air. Though the building was three floors high, the owners had ripped out the separation between the second and third floors, leaving a tall ceiling and a stunning view of the city below. Tables and chairs sprinkled the room, and chatty occupants filled them all to capacity. The bar was easy to identify from across the room since it had been backed by thick wooden paneling extending to the third-floor ceiling. Glass shelves lined the wood, and the bottles of bourbon sitting on top of them were backlit by recessed lights.

"I think we've found the place to be in Amberley," Anna said.

Oliver had grown used to large crowds when he lived in the city, but much time had passed since he'd been in a place filled from wall to wall with people. The crowd seemed to pulse, and he was somewhat overwhelmed. He backed toward the staircase, but before he could escape, Anna grabbed him by the arm and pulled him through a narrow pathway toward the bar.

"Come on," she said.

"There's no place to sit." He peered at the bar ahead of him.

"Just follow me. That couple's about to get up. They've just paid."

Sure enough, a man and woman rose from their seats as they made it to the bar, leaving two vacant barstools behind.

Anna rushed in and grabbed the seats, mean-mugging two girls who approached from the other side.

"Perfect," she said.

Oliver gave an apologetic smile to the girls, but they had already set their sights on two other seats across the room.

"Come on, sit down," Anna said. "You've got to be aggressive, or you'll be standing all night."

"You sure fit in here awfully well for having spent your entire life in Christchurch."

"People are the same everywhere. Sometimes, you have to assert yourself. And just because I live in Christchurch doesn't mean I'm a shut-in."

After looking through the extensive binder of drinks, they both settled on Manhattans, which arrived with delicately spiraled orange peels and toothpicks with smoked cherries.

"What do we toast to?" Oliver asked.

"You've been in Christchurch for nearly a year now, right? How about that?"

"All right, to one year in Christchurch," he replied, lifting his martini glass and clinking the edge against hers.

"And to a successful day at the flea," she added, clinking his glass once more.

The bourbon burned Oliver's throat, and he tried

hard not to make a face as Anna took a drink of hers without so much as a shudder.

"So, your mommy issues aside, do you still like it in Christchurch? Are you getting tired of us yet?"

"Are you kidding? The last year has been a blast. Plus, I could never leave Pan behind," he said.

"Hey!" Anna feigned offense and kicked him under the table.

"I'm just joking! I love it at the bakery with you two. Never thought I'd end up here, but I'm happy I did."

He still thought of Briarwood often when he sat out back and looked upon the forest that housed the invisible village. Simon's son had never popped up in Christchurch, and Oliver hoped he'd found a place to call home far away from the small cell that had held him for so long.

"What about you?" he asked. "Any big plans on the horizon?"

"You're looking at them," she said, tipping her glass toward him.

Deep into the second Manhattan and a few slices of pizza, Anna looked at her watch. "I think two drinks is enough for me. What's next? It is a Saturday night, after all."

Oliver thought for a minute and pulled a folded piece of paper from his pocket. "I saved one of these from last week. We still have twenty minutes to make it to Pearl's House of Dead Things, or whatever it's called," he said sarcastically. "Could be entertaining."

"The dead-bat puppet show? We have to!" Anna tipped her glass back and finished the rest of her drink.

CHAPTER FIVE

The temperature had dropped several degrees since the sun sank behind the Amberley skyline. Anna and Oliver walked the block in search of the church Ruby had mentioned the week before. Once they spotted the steeple in the distance, they traced the streets until they found the church's main entrance. After that, they circled the building until they found the mysterious venue listed on the flyer.

The destination was easy to spot, thanks to a sign reading The Parlor hanging from a lamppost at the base of the steps. A Ouija-board planchette was etched underneath the name, with an eye watching from the circular letter window. The building itself sat slightly recessed between the two neighboring homes as if trying to conceal its secrets from passersby. Thick crimson drapes hung in the front windows, making it impossible to see inside. The building trim was painted black and the brick a dark green, in odd contrast to the colorful houses around it.

Oliver had seen plenty of houses like this before, but all of them lived on-screen in the macabre movies he would force Izzy to watch, and all of them contained monsters.

He gripped the handle of the wrought-iron fence and pushed, and the hinges let out a loud squeal as they entered the front courtyard. They climbed the brick steps to the large carved wooden door, and he tugged at the antique knob, but the entrance was locked tight. He looked back at Anna, second-guessing his eagerness to see whatever waited on the other side.

"Ring the bell," she said, gesturing for him to go ahead. "This has to be the place."

He pressed the black button on the doorframe, and a low-pitched chime echoed through the house. The door opened immediately, causing him to jump as a lanky girl returned to her stool on the other side of the door. Her black velvet blouse with white collar and black ribbon reminded Oliver of an old schoolgirl uniform. The smell of burning sage wafted through the doorway.

"Here for the show?" she asked in monotone.

"Absolutely," Oliver replied.

"You're just in time. That'll be twenty for each of you," she said as if she'd said it a thousand times before.

Oliver peered into the room ahead of them. The light from the dim wall lanterns flickered off the dark wallpaper, and several skeletal bats hung from the ceiling over the entryway, posed in midflight. People were gathered in the room next to them—a room lined with framed taxidermy, obscure artwork, and jarred oddities.

"It includes a discount on a reading too," the girl added as if it would push him over the edge.

Oliver reached for his wallet and pulled out two twenties. When Anna saw this, she pushed by him.

"No, no. I'll pay for myself," she said, pulling cash from her purse and giving a cheery smile to the girl at the door.

The girl handed Anna and Oliver two pins, fashioned to look like the planchette on the sign. "Wear these while you're here. They showed you've paid. Welcome to the Grim Menagerie." She gave a lackluster wave toward the room ahead.

They followed a trail of people to the lounge next to the entryway. A group gathered around a bar, where a man with a long brown ponytail poured samples of a pear-colored liquid into fancy shot glasses. Others walked the walls, taking in the obscure framed artwork and dead dioramas.

Anna gave Oliver a hard jab in the rib. "Look at that!" She pointed up at the ceiling.

They were standing directly underneath a large chandelier made entirely of bones. The piece was massive, with rows of what he hoped were animal leg bones dangling freely. Hip bones formed decorative flowers at the ends of each radial column, and each bloom held a flickering candle.

"I've never seen anything like that. It's gruesome," he said.

"But oddly beautiful," Anna added. "Must have taken forever to build."

Anna wandered to the other corner of the room. "I think I found a gift idea for Izzy." She pointed at a taxidermic cat, which had been outfitted in a baker's hat and apron. The animal was carefully balancing a small pie on top of a serving tray.

As Oliver leaned in for a closer look, he realized the small object sticking out of the pie was the rear end of a mouse, its squiggly tail twisted into a curlicue.

He noticed the price tag hanging from the chef's hat. "It's for sale. Bet Izzy would never speak to us again if we brought this home."

"Just hope kitty died of natural causes," Anna said.

"An unfortunate run-in with a car, actually," someone said from behind.

Oliver and Anna turned to see Ruby leaning over them.

"Good to see you again—Oliver and Anna, right?"

"You've got a good memory," Anna replied.

"This business requires that I maintain excellent relationships with both the living and the dead," she said with a smirk. "So, would you like to take Midnight here home with you?"

"Midnight?"

"She was a lovely cat—always hung round the alley next to the shop. It's a pity, really."

"You stuffed your pet?" Oliver asked.

"She didn't belong to anyone. She was her own cat. And what better way to honor the dead than to immortalize them?"

He wasn't sure how to respond, but fortunately, the man serving drinks at the bar was waving to get Ruby's attention.

"Got to run," she said. "Hope you enjoy the show." She paced out of the room and into the hallway.

"If I could have everyone's attention, please!" the man shouted. "My name's Caleb, and I'm happy to welcome you to the Grim Menagerie. The show is about to begin. Please follow our lovely guide, Jen, to the stage."

Jen, the same person who'd enthusiastically

greeted them at the door, gave a half-hearted wave and steered the crowd toward the back of the house.

The hallway led to a large open room, and the crowd shuffled to fill several rows of chairs in the back. A wooden stage sat at the front, bordered with several large boxlike shapes concealed under thick sheets. A hexagonal wooden table sat in the center of the stage, complete with a perfectly polished crystal ball in the center. A large panel draped with a forest-green curtain served as the backdrop for the table scene.

"This ought to be interesting," Oliver said.

Once the crowd had settled in, Jen pulled a curtain over the doorway and approached a record player at the back of the room. Instead of setting the needle on the outer edge of the black vinyl, she set it at the center. The room filled with the sound of the needle scratching against the end of the record, bouncing back and forth against the hard stop.

"That's my favorite song," Oliver joked, but before he could see Anna's reaction, the room went black.

Several audience members gasped, and even Anna, who wasn't scared of anything, shuffled in her chair.

"The dead are always speaking," Ruby said from the back of the room. "But only a select few have the ability to hear them." As she spoke, she walked to the stage, her thick heels thunking across the floor. "And even fewer can serve as a conduit between the worlds of the living and the dead—can permit ordinary souls to hear the other realm. Fortunately, you happen to be in the presence of one of these select few." She took a seat at the table, directly behind the crystal ball.

"So, I'll ask: are there any spirits who have a message for us this evening?"

Anna was looking at Oliver out of the corner of her eye.

A low moan emerged over the record-player static.

"Looks like we have a taker. Sometimes, we have to give them a medium, like a tone or sound. Kind of like dialing in a radio station. Once we've found a spirit, we can channel them through the crystal."

The scene might have been a rehearsed act by an experienced huckster, but ever since Oliver had seen the death and destruction caused by the Briarwood Witch, any mention of supernatural phenomena made his stomach churn.

"Do you have something to tell us?" Ruby asked.

The gleam was subtle at first. A light from the center of the crystal sphere cast a dim glow on her face. As the groan from the record-player speakers grew louder, so did the pulsing light.

"Do you have a message you would like to share?"

The groan grew louder, and the table began to shake.

"She's probably just doing that with her knees," Anna whispered, almost in the form of a question.

Suddenly, the table shot up from the floor, rising several feet above Ruby's head.

The crowd gasped.

"Control yourself!" she commanded. "What do you have to say? We are listening."

The table came crashing to the floor, barely missing Ruby, although the woman sat confidently in her chair without so much as a flinch. The crystal ball hung in the air, and the sphere gave off a white-hot burst of light as the record-player groan grew to a full-blown scream.

"Help me!" The voice blasted from the speakers, and the crystal exploded into sparkling glass-like confetti. The needle scratched across the record as the room went dark again.

The shriek was too much for one of the audience members behind Oliver, and she let out a scream of her own.

The house lights rose, illuminating Ruby on the stage, but the table and crystal ball were now firmly back in place as if nothing had happened to them.

The terrified woman in the audience stood plastered against the back wall of the room as her date tried to comfort her. As the crowd turned to watch the hysterics, their attention proved too much for her, and she bolted through the closed curtain into the hallway.

"Some are not ready to hear from the other side," Ruby said. "Better she leaves now since it only gets worse from here. My, the spirits are loud tonight." The crowd gave a nervous laugh. "But what if we could do more than hear the spirits of the dead? What if we could see them, even bring them back to visit?"

She crossed the stage toward one of the covered rectangles.

"Before zoos, there were menageries—small collections of animals assembled and maintained by rich aristocrats. As these menageries grew in popularity from the seventeen hundreds to eighteen hundreds, a few savvy entrepreneurs started their own traveling shows, and these eventually morphed into the circuses we know today. But not all cared about the creatures they held in captivity. Many abused animals, which often died from malnourishment and mistreatment. When we constructed our own little menagerie, we decided to celebrate those unfortunate souls that were victims of their times."

With a dramatic flourish, she ripped the curtain away from one of the containers. A red glow flashed across the gallery. The container appeared to be a glass aquarium filled with a phosphorescent liquid.

Oliver's heart dropped. He had seen this color

before, and he still had nightmares about the one-eyed witch who'd come with it. The tank was filled with the blood of the boy who'd escaped to the woods a year before, the same blood that had flowed above the atrium in the Briarwood town hall. This blood could heal wounds, rejuvenate aged bodies, and apparently bring animals back to life, and it belonged to Simon's son.

Anna grabbed his arm.

Several skeletal fish crisscrossed the tank, gliding through the swirling reds and oranges.

"The Hindus believe animals have souls, too, and we wondered if we could call an animal's soul back to its body." Ruby reached for the curtain on the next tank and pulled it loose, letting the fabric slowly cascade to the floor. The tank was tall, taller than Ruby, in fact. The tree inside the display looked as if someone had taken a massive oak and shrunk it down. The branches were barren, and blood submerged the entire scene.

Instead of fish, this display featured birds. The skeletal figures hopped from branch to branch—little zombie parakeets in an undead aquarium.

"Unfortunately, they don't sing like they used to."

Ruby beckoned for Jen at the back of the room. She joined Ruby on stage and helped push the large covered backdrop forward until it came within a few feet of the front row of seats. She angled it down at the audience.

"And you may think this display morbid, but aren't we all just walking skeletons? Spirits-to-be?"

With a snap at the back of the sheet, the curtain fell to the floor, revealing a massive mirror underneath. The surface reflected the audience, and Oliver saw his own likeness looking back at him. But instead of being peach fleshed and full of life, the reflection was that of a corpse, skin dull and shrunken. The entire audience, for that matter, looked like zombies.

Oliver's heart raced, and the rest of the crowd muttered amongst themselves. He touched his face, and the figure on the other side of the mirror did the same.

"But it's best not to dwell too long on the future. And maybe it's all just a parlor trick."

She snapped her fingers, and the image on the mirror flashed. The figures on the other side returned to normal, and Oliver recognized himself sitting in the audience.

The crowd erupted into nervous applause.

Ruby stood at the front of the stage and bowed.

"Can you believe that?" Anna asked. "I nearly had a panic attack."

"We have to talk to her," Oliver said. "Simon's son is here."

"Please, stay and have a look at our wonderful creatures. We hope to add more to our collection, so tell your friends and family about our gruesome little show. And those who'd like a personal reading can make their way back to my study."

Ruby hopped down from the stage and walked toward the front of the house while those in the crowd made their way to the tanks. They seemed to be looking for proof the undead animals were all some elaborate illusion. But Oliver knew otherwise. Somehow, Simon's son had made it to Amberley, and his blood must have been even more powerful than Oliver had imagined.

Oliver and Anna pushed their way toward the front of the house, where a line had already formed next to the closed door of the study. Caleb stood at the front of the line, taking cash from the first set of reading seekers.

"We should just go. Clearly, he's still alive, so we know he survived. Let's leave him alone," Anna said in a low voice.

"We don't know that. How do we know they aren't mistreating him? What if they're abusing him the same way Simon did? Don't you remember how he looked, slumped over in the chair and dripping blood? They filled entire tanks with his blood, like the pool in Christchurch. They can't be his friends."

"Fine, but what are we going to do? Break him out of here?"

"I need to know he's all right."

"That'll be twenty, each," Caleb said without looking up, when they finally reached the front of the line.

Once they had paid, Caleb opened the door into Ruby's study. Dark wainscoting bordered the walls, which were a deep green. Fringed cloth covered a small wooden table that sat under an old chandelier. Ruby sat at the table, sipping from a delicate floral teacup.

"Hope you enjoyed the show. Please, come in and have a seat," she said as Anna and Oliver entered. "How can I help you?"

Oliver wasted no time getting to the point. "We know how you filled those tanks. Where is he?" He noticed a glimmer of discomfort in Ruby's eye, which she quickly covered with a slight shake of the head.

"I'm afraid I don't know who you're talking about," she replied.

"He came here a year ago, didn't he? Probably acted as if he'd come from another place and time—like he was crazy. His father had been abusing him, and his arms were covered with scars. And you have tanks filled with his blood on your stage."

Ruby drained the rest of her tea then stood up.

"Clearly, tonight's events have caused you great stress. It may be best if you leave and take time to calm yourself." She walked toward Oliver and placed her hand on his shoulder.

"We helped him escape and just want to make sure he's all right," he said, jerking away.

Ruby bowed her head and clenched her fist as if mulling over the request.

"There are too many people here now. Come back tomorrow afternoon, and maybe I can help you. Now, I'll have to move on to the next guest." She ushered them to the door. As Oliver stepped through, she grabbed his arm. "I can guarantee he's happier now than he's ever been. We are not taking advantage of him."

"We'll see about that," he replied as he pulled his arm away.

The line for readings had wrapped down the hallway and around the entryway. Oliver pushed through to reach the exit, and Anna followed suit.

"What's going on in there?" she asked once they reached the street. "Think she was really talking with the dead?"

"I don't know," he replied. "But those tanks weren't an illusion. What are you doing tomorrow afternoon?"

"What do you think I'm doing tomorrow afternoon? You're not coming back here alone. You can't have all the fun."

They walked toward the parking lot and drove Izzy's car back to Christchurch. The ride was silent as both Anna and Oliver struggled to make sense of what they'd just seen.

CHAPTER SIX

Oliver stood over the metal kitchen table, scowling at a lump of dough, which slumped sadly in front of him.

"Why does the dough hate me today?" he asked.

Izzy poked her head out from behind a metal rack. She walked to the table and poked the flat, sad mess. "Too much yeast. It's collapsed in on itself."

Oliver had slowly been "helping" more and more in the kitchen, but he was fairly certain he was doing more harm than good. Although he'd made substantial progress on the business side of the house, Izzy insisted baking skills were essential for anyone having anything to do with running a bakery.

"You have to know the dough before you can sell the dough." She slid the collapsed lump into the garbage.

He'd managed muffins and cookies, but bread dough had proven to be his nemesis. Fortunately, flour was cheap, which eased his fear of single-handedly bringing the bakery to financial ruin.

Although his baking skills still needed work, Oliver had introduced Izzy to the novel concepts of spreadsheets and the World Wide Web. He'd made the mistake of helping her file her taxes, and her accounting system consisted of scraps of paper kept in a cardboard box under the table in the bakery kitchen. He had no clue how she had kept the business afloat for so long. In the last year, he'd also created a small website, and they were even receiving honey orders online. In the past month, they had sold more honey on the Web and at the Amberley Flea than they had in the bakery.

"Hey, who is the baking expert in the room?" Izzy raised her hand at her own question. "So who is more likely to be right about bakery-related miscellanea?" She kept her hand in the air.

Oliver rolled his eyes.

"Now, give me a hand with these tables. If you and Anna are planning on heading to Amberley this afternoon, we'll need to make sure everything is ready for the council meeting."

"I'm sorry to leave you hanging."

"Don't be. I can't imagine what that poor boy has gone through."

Although Izzy was one of the most carefree people he'd ever known, she had a worried look on her face that made him uncomfortable.

"What's wrong?" he asked as they scooted several square tables together.

"Are you sure you can trust these people? What if they're waiting for you and Anna to show up alone? What if they've done something terrible to that boy?"

Oliver hadn't stopped to consider the possibility. *What if they are waiting for us?* "I'll write down the address, and you can call the police if we're not back by sundown."

"I'm sure it's fine. I'm just being silly." She shook her head. "With all these witches and evildoers running about, my senses are all out of sorts."

"We'll be careful."

"Good. I don't know what I would do without you and Anna. I would have to teach Pan to bake, and that would tough, considering the little guy doesn't have thumbs."

"You could always ask Bev to help you." He grinned.

"Speaking of Bev, I don't suppose you've told her about your little adventure in Amberley or anything related to Briarwood, have you?" She rested her palms on one of the tables and looked up at him.

"Mom has a hard enough time accepting that I've moved off into the country to bake. I think we can omit the terrifying supernatural elements from our conversations for now."

Izzy and Oliver pulled the remaining tables out from the booths and bumped them up together for the council brainstorming session. She'd offered the bakery as a place to discuss the upcoming fundraiser while the council's typical meeting spot at the town hall was being repainted.

The plan was to host a music night at The Horseman and to use the funds to replace the aging sidewalks around the square and repair the uneven bricks next to the fountain. After Widow Morgan nearly broke a hip on her afternoon stroll a few weeks before, the Elders decided something had to be done.

Izzy needed the car for a few afternoon deliveries, so Oliver and Anna walked to Christchurch station as soon as they'd wrapped up at the bakery.

"I think Izzy expects someone to murder us," Oliver said as they boarded the train.

"Thanks for putting that thought into my head," Anna replied.

"Just letting you know, if things go south, you will have to defend us both. I'm not a fighter." He laughed.

"If things go south, you better hope you can run faster than I can. That's all that matters."

Amberley's train station reminded Oliver of the one back in the city. Old bits of gum speckled the dirty tile, trash cans overflowed, and people sat in the corners with cardboard signs asking for spare change.

They took the street exit and headed in The Parlor's direction.

"Talk to your mom at all today?" Anna asked.

"A bit. The first thing she asked was why I was out so late last night. I was tempted to tell her the truth, just to see her reaction. She seems to have eased up a little, though. I think the time in the bakery may have convinced her I'm working hard."

"Sounds like she's coming around," Anna replied.

Although the streets had been filled the previous night, the evening crooners were nowhere to be found, and Oliver assumed the college students were still in bed, sleeping off hangovers.

The daylight revealed details about The Parlor that had been hidden in the darkness. The house's shingles shimmered like scales in the sun, and intricate wooden flourishes lined the box-gutter borders. The building still held its eerie charm, but the sunlight revealed a house that had been deeply cared for by its owners.

As they approached the front gate, Oliver heard a rustling from the alley next to them. He peered around the corner and noticed a man hunched over one of the open trash cans. The man nearly lost his balance as he teetered over the edge and fished for some unknown buried treasure. After a few moments, he emerged victorious, holding two crumpled aluminum cans, which he dropped into the plastic bag next to him. Although the man stepped back from the can, the hunch remained, his head nearly at the same level as his waist.

Oliver couldn't look away before accidentally catching the man's eye. He hobbled toward Oliver and Anna, his oversized wool sweater stained with evidence of his regular dumpster dives. He wore strapped sandals, and the nails of his clubbed toes hung awkwardly over the edges as if his feet were slowly absorbing the leather.

Anna tugged at Oliver's arm, but the man gave a wave and a cheery snaggletoothed grin that made him feel guilty for turning away.

"Hey there," the man said.

"Hey," Oliver said, returning the wave.

Upon closer inspection, he saw the man had a nearly full set of teeth, blackened and worn down to the gums. His breath carried through the air and hit Oliver's nose, the fetid stench nearly knocking him backward.

"You shouldn't go in there," he said. "Full of

demons, that place." He pointed at The Parlor's entrance.

"Oh, really?" Anna replied, feigning worry. "What kind of demons?"

"They bring the dead back to life in there. Very dark stuff."

"We'll be careful," Anna replied.

"Very dark stuff," he said again, more to himself than to Anna and Oliver.

"Thanks for the warning," Oliver added.

"I used to play Paganini, you know—the 'Devil's Laughter.'" The man hummed to himself and fluttered his fingers as if he were playing an invisible violin. He turned his back to them and stumbled around the alleyway to the melody.

"Let's go before he comes back," Anna said under her breath.

"He's harmless."

"Well, we don't have an hour to stand and talk to him." She gestured toward the staircase.

The two climbed the stairs and rang the doorbell. Jen must have been off for the morning because Caleb greeted them at the door.

"Help you?" he asked.

"We're here to see Ruby. She told us to swing by this afternoon," Oliver said.

"Oh, of course." Caleb opened the door the rest of the way and welcomed them inside.

The place felt even larger than it had before, since the crowd had dispersed. Ruby sat at the lounge bar, hunched over a teacup. Her face appeared even paler than before.

Caleb turned the corner into the lounge. "Your guests are here."

"Gah! Not so loud," Ruby replied. She didn't turn to acknowledge them but instead beckoned them with a half-hearted wave. "Come join me."

Anna and Oliver pulled up barstools next to her.

Ruby rested her head in her hands and massaged her temples. She seemed to forget Oliver and Anna were sitting next to her.

"Thanks for letting us come today," Oliver said after a moment of awkward silence.

"Like a cup?" she asked, pointing at her flower teacup.

"Oh, no thank you," Oliver replied.

"Sure, why not?" Anna added.

"Caleb, another cup please," she said loudly.

A few moments later, Caleb returned and placed a teacup in front of Anna.

"Thank you." Anna lifted the drink to her nose and choked on the smell. "It's whiskey."

"How insulting. It's cognac," Ruby corrected,

"from my personal bar. I don't drink the swill we serve to customers."

"Early, don't you think?" Anna asked.

"What do you want with Asher?" Ruby asked, ignoring the criticism.

"Asher?" Oliver asked. "That's his name?"

Ruby looked up from her drink. "You mean to tell me you never learned his name? You know who I'm referring to—the man I found stumbling through the streets a year ago, muttering insanity about his father being chased out of some imaginary town. He promised me a handsome sum if I helped him find his way back. I had no clue what the hell he was going on about, and he couldn't seem to remember from which direction he'd come. I thought he was a heroin addict at first, and so did everyone else who passed him by. He acted as if he'd never seen a city before, like he'd dropped out of the sky and everything was new to him. He looked like someone had tortured him."

"So he told you about Briarwood?" Oliver asked.

"He was shell-shocked at first but opened up once he realized he was safe. Unfortunately, the only experience he seems to have is confined to whatever cell he was locked up in. He refuses to come out of the goddamn basement most of the time—says he likes it down there."

"What about the blood? How did you find out?" Oliver asked.

"He told us after we noticed the scars. Naturally, I asked why the hell he'd sliced his arm up several hundred times."

"And you believed him?" Anna asked.

"Darling, have you seen the show? He's not the only one around here with *unusual* talents." Ruby pointed at the empty teacup in front of her and swirled her index finger. The cup jiggled at first, then two small porcelain legs shot out from underneath. The cup ran across the bar, past Oliver and Anna, and promptly jumped off the edge, like a lemming hurling itself off the side of a cliff. Oliver and Anna stared down at the pile, unable to process what they had just seen.

"Only thing is," Ruby said, "what Asher can do is real. All I have are illusions."

Oliver looked up at Ruby, who sat in front of the same empty teacup that had just committed porcelain suicide. He looked down to where the cup had fallen and found no evidence of the broken shards that had been there just a moment before.

Anna lifted her cup and downed the contents with a single swallow.

"So I can relate to the man. He's been punished for

something he can't control and abused so that others could take advantage of his unique abilities."

"But *you're* using his blood in your shows," Oliver added. "Isn't that taking advantage of him?"

"He insisted and even tried to get me to use it on myself. Lord knows I could use it. Those big illusions take it right out of me. He wanted to contribute, and we allowed it, but we won't use his blood on ourselves. That's out of the question. Unnaturals shouldn't take advantage of each other."

"Unnaturals? What are you talking about?"

"Self-explanatory, isn't it? People with abilities normal society would refer to as unnatural. The most common is telekinesis, but it manifests itself differently in everyone. Runs in family lines, but there seems to be no rhyme or reason who in the family gets it."

"There are more people like you and Asher?" Oliver asked.

"You don't really think Asher and I are the only two in the world with this condition and we just happened to cross paths, do you, darling? There are people like us all over the place. I've never seen another Unnatural like him, though. He's a walking, talking fountain of youth."

"I've heard nothing like this before. How can so many people exist without being noticed?"

"You think we're eager to be discovered?

Remember the Witch Trials? See how Asher has been treated? No, most of us like to keep quiet. Sure, an occasional mishap makes the news, but it's a rare exception."

"But anyone who wanders into The Parlor sees what you're capable of—the mirror and dead animals."

"Parlor tricks. Perhaps some think I can really channel the dead, which I can't, but most assume they're being tricked. That's what they pay for. Everyone loves a good magic show."

How many people like Ruby and Asher have I come into contact with without even realizing?

He could see the exhaustion in Ruby's eyes and wondered how much of it was because of the use of her powers and how much came from trying to survive in a world that saw her as unnatural.

"Does Asher know his father's dead?" The question had been percolating in the back of Oliver's head.

Ruby slumped over her teacup. "Shit. No. What happened?"

"Age. They carted him off to jail without Asher's blood to keep him going. The man might have been one hundred years old, for all we know."

"He seems to be coming around. We've had a few conversations about his father, and he gets the man was a murderer. He understands how abusive Simon was to his sister and to him, but I don't know how he'll handle his father's death. His sister's was hard enough."

"Can we see him?" Oliver asked.

Ruby hesitated for a moment. "He may not react kindly to you. He's mentioned the man who tried to kill his father—I assume that's you—and even though he's come a long way, I'm sure he's still got hostility hidden away somewhere."

"What if we promise to leave right away if seeing us is too much for him?" Anna added.

"Why do you want to see him, anyway?"

Oliver had been asked this question several times, but he still wasn't able to articulate the real answer.

"We want to see for ourselves that he's all right," Anna replied when Oliver couldn't.

"I'll take you to the basement," Ruby said. "Just take it slow and don't mention his father's death. I'll break *that* news later."

As they walked through the house to the kitchen, a foul smell punched Oliver in the nose. Caleb stood over a stockpot, swirling its boiling contents with a large wooden spoon.

"Chicken bones for a new display piece," he said, seeing the disgusted looks on Anna's and Oliver's faces.

"Why are you boiling them?" Anna asked.

"Removes the last bits of flesh," he replied, as if the answer should have been obvious. "Trying to convince

Ruby here to let me buy dermestid beetles. They do the same thing but without the wonderful aroma. Plus, it would be nice to have some *live* pets around the house."

"Gross," Anna replied.

"He can't even take care of the taxidermy properly, and he expects me to let him have live things?" Ruby smirked at Caleb. "You saw what happened to our cat."

The door to the basement sat behind the kitchen pantry, and Ruby ushered Oliver and Anna inside.

The stairwell was long and narrow, and if Ruby had resolved to murder them, this would have been the place to do it. That fear had been pushed out of Oliver's mind, though, since he'd had a chance to talk to her.

They descended the rickety staircase and came to a slender wooden door at its base. Oliver tapped the door with his knuckle.

"Come in," someone replied from the other side.

The doorway led to a workshop of sorts, a surprisingly finished basement for the style of house it occupied. Shelves contained jars of metal fasteners, nails, and screws, along with obscure materials like animal skins and bones. The far corner of the room held a small living area with a bed and a dated mustard-colored sofa. Bookshelves lined the side walls and overflowed to where stacks of books sat piled on the floor next to them. Asher stood over a large workbench, his back to the door.

"You know this set you gave me is incomplete. It's missing a femur," he said as he spun around, holding a handful of small animal bones. He wore a green-striped shirt with an olive vest and maroon pants. His brown hair was curly and sprang back and forth against his forehead. He looked different from the scared blood-soaked man who'd cowered behind Izzy's sofa the year before.

When Asher saw Oliver, his expression immediately soured into a mix of anger and fear.

"What are you doing here?" he asked with a quivering voice.

To make sure you're okay? The reasoning seemed flimsy.

"Get out!" Asher shouted, not waiting for a reply.

"We—" Oliver began, but Asher picked up a heavy metal tool and held it in the air, threatening to fling it at them.

"Okay, okay," Oliver said, holding a hand out and backing toward the door. Anna didn't need a second warning and had already made her way halfway up the stairs by the time Oliver hit the bottom step.

Ruby was standing in the kitchen, talking to Caleb. "Didn't go well, did it?" she asked as Oliver emerged from the staircase, face flushed and lungs short of breath.

He shook his head.

"Was afraid of that," Ruby replied. "Still has a bit of loyalty to his dad, and you are somewhat responsible for separating the two. Wait till I tell him the man's dead."

"Stockholm syndrome," Caleb added, still monitoring the large stockpot.

"Go have a seat, and I'll see if I can calm him down," Ruby said.

Anna and Oliver headed back to the lounge bar and waited.

"We should go. He clearly doesn't want us here," Anna said. "We're only going to make things worse."

"Let's give it a second. He'll come around eventually," Oliver replied.

"Maybe, but how do you think he will react when he finds out his father is dead?"

Oliver shrugged.

They sat at the lounge bar, making small talk for some time, waiting to see if Asher would emerge from the basement.

"I've been told my father is responsible for murder."

Asher's voice caught them by surprise, and both

Anna and Oliver twisted around in their barstools to see him standing in the doorway. His eyes shifted from side to side as if waiting for someone to pounce since he'd left the safety of the basement. "If this is true, he deserved to be carted away. I apologize for how I reacted to you. You were simply protecting your family. But he is my father. He may have kept me locked away, but he cared for me, so forgive me if I cannot so easily forgive you."

Sure, he cared for your when he wasn't cutting you open and drinking your blood.

As Asher approached them, Oliver noticed a gold chain around his neck, shimmering in the sunlight. The round edge of a tarnished gold coin peeked out from behind the top of his shirt.

"Is that the key to Briarwood?" Oliver asked.

Asher didn't seem to understand.

"The coin—did you get that from your father?" he clarified.

Asher pulled the chain out above his shirt, revealing the familiar crow with thorns underneath. "It fell from his pocket when he tumbled down the stairs that night. I'd planned to give it back to him, but he crashed into the statue. I thought the men were coming to kill us, so I ran for the woods. Caleb made it into a necklace for me."

"Have you been back to Briarwood?"

"No, no I couldn't. I'm sure they'd kill me if I went

back. I probably couldn't find the town again, even if I wanted to."

Oliver had assumed the coin had gone with Simon and had been locked away in a prison somewhere, probably lost forever with the man's passing. Most nights, he would look down across the field at the briars and wonder if the town had somehow re-established order. He thought of Gideon and the agony Mercy's death must have caused him and wondered if the man was doing all right. He assumed he'd never be able to cross the patch again.

"So you like it here?" Anna asked.

Asher looked at Ruby, who had entered the lounge from the hallway. "They treat me like an equal. They let me be a part of this." He gestured around the room.

"You are an equal," Ruby added. "The whole idea for the menagerie was yours. You should show them what you're working on for next weekend. The new exhibit will make the fish tank and birdcage seem dull."

Asher's eyes darted to Oliver and Anna before shifting to Ruby. "But it's a secret," he said.

"Go ahead." Ruby waved him on. "I'm sure they'll promise not to go spoiling the show by telling anyone else."

"We swear," Oliver said. "We'll even bring a new customer next weekend. The show would be right up my great aunt's obscure alley." *Probably too much for Mom, though.*

Asher led Oliver and Anna back down the stairs to his workshop.

"We wanted to try with a larger animal," he said as he opened the door of a large wooden cabinet hanging above the workbench. He retrieved a wide glass jar filled with swirling blood and set it in front of them. A pile of bones sat on the far end of the workbench, and Asher carefully scooped them up and set them down next to the container.

Oliver had never seen Asher's blood up close before. Tiny glitter-like particles zipped around the container like microscopic schools of fish.

"So it never dries?" Oliver asked.

"Only when it's been used to heal, I think," Asher replied.

Oliver rubbed his side where Simon had jabbed his slender cane blade. Asher's blood had fizzled over his wound until it had completely healed the gash.

"Doesn't that wear you out, though—losing enough blood to fill a container like that?"

"For a little while, but it regenerates quickly. I can barely even feel the needle anymore, especially after filling the glass tanks upstairs, and you remember Father's atrium."

Asher's blood had filled a swirling pool above the atrium in Briarwood. That must have taken years.

"And the needle is much better than the scarificator. Ruby tells me people do it all the time here. She called it 'giving blood,' I think."

Oliver remembered the small metal box with protruding blades that Simon had used to slice Asher's arms open. Mercy told him it had been used for medical purposes, but it looked like a torture device. The thought of Simon using it on Asher made Oliver shiver.

"Stand back a little, if you will," Asher said, ensuring a foot of clearance between them and the bench.

Asher picked up some bones and dumped them into the specimen jar. "This works best when we have a complete set. I'm not sure why, but we discovered that with the fish."

He swept the rest of the bones off the table and into his cupped palm then dropped them into the jar. The bones hit the surface of the liquid with several small plops.

"What kind of animal is it?" Oliver asked.

The bones were larger than bird bones and too large to belong to fish.

"Just wait a moment, and you'll see." Asher knelt down so he was eye level with the large jar.

At first, the bones sat motionless at the bottom, aside from a few bubbles of trapped air escaping to the surface. Then the pile wiggled as if the blood was beginning to boil. Bubbles formed at the bottom of the jar and floated to the top, and one by one, the bones popped away from the pile and into position, suspended in the liquid. Instead of floating independently, they seemed to move in perfect unison, eventually forming the outline of an articulated animal skeleton. The creature hunched on all fours as what appeared to be a tail wrapped around the side of the jar. At first, Oliver thought it might have been a cat, but once the creature's skull popped into place and the animal was fully formed, it sat back on its hind legs and pressed its front paws on the sides of the glass.

"A monkey?" Oliver asked.

"A rhesus, to be precise," Asher corrected.

The monkey twisted its head and swished its arms through the liquid as if trying to comprehend why it had woken up underwater.

"Why is it still a skeleton? If the blood can heal wounds, why don't they fill in and become full animals again?"

"I don't have an answer for that, I'm afraid. We've only tried this with bones. Maybe because there's no flesh left to regenerate or maybe because the animals have long been dead. They don't seem to use up the blood, so maybe once something is dead, it's impossible to fully bring it back. We started with the fish, and they've been swimming around for weeks."

"But surely, he's not alive. How could he think without a brain?"

"It seems the bones have their own memories. We've been trying to get a few of these ready for the show, but do you know how difficult it is to find complete monkey skeletons in the city?" Asher asked.

"It's a real problem in this day and age," Anna said sarcastically.

"The monkeys are more vicious too," Asher said.

"What do you mean?" Oliver asked.

Using a knuckle, Asher tapped on the side of the jar. The monkey, which had been miming his away around the glass jar, snapped his head toward his finger and bared its fangs. The animal reared up on its hind legs and sprang toward them, leaping out above the crest of the blood at the top of the jar. Oliver stepped backward and shielded his face from the impending zombie-monkey bite. As soon as the animal hit the air, the creature collapsed, and bones flew everywhere, splattering the three with blood. Asher laughed and started to collect the bones that had fallen to the floor, while Oliver stood frozen in a mix of disgust and fear. The bones seemed to vibrate in Asher's hand, still somewhat energized by the splatters of blood but unable to support themselves without the aid of the liquid.

"And there you see our problem."

"What are you going to do?" Oliver asked.

Asher walked to one of the metal shelves across the room and returned with a heavy metal lid and clamp. He dropped the bones back into the liquid and set the lid on top of the jar, snapping the metal clamp in place. "Just have to make sure they have no way to get out. We can't go splattering blood all over the audience. It might be hard to keep the crowd coming."

"I've never seen something like that before," Oliver said, pointing at the lid of the glass jar. "What is it?"

"This is a large specimen jar. They typically use these to preserve medical oddities and animals, like fetal calves."

"Gross," Anna said.

"A fetal calf is gross, but you're perfectly fine with a reanimated monkey in a large jar of blood?" Oliver asked.

"Fair point," Anna replied.

"You never know. People will pay good money for a scare." Oliver added. "Maybe you should leave the lid off."

"You should have seen it when we first tried the fish without a lid. Took hours to clean up."

As Asher mopped the floor, Oliver asked something that had been on his mind since he first saw the aquarium of swirling blood. "They're not forcing you to do this, are they? They're not keeping you here against your will?"

Asher bristled at the questions. "Forcing me? No, nothing like that. Ruby could barely pay rent when I arrived. Still, she and Caleb opened their home to me, fed me, and clothed me. The least I could do was offer my little talent to say thank you. They refused at first, but I insisted. And they hardly keep me confined. In fact, they've been trying to get me to leave the house for some time. I find it more comfortable down here, with my books. Reminds me of home."

"Minus the bars," Anna added.

In some ways, Ruby and Caleb had treated Asher like Izzy had treated Oliver, with unquestioning kindness.

After Asher cleaned up the mess, he walked Anna and Oliver to the front door.

"I hope to see you at next week's show," Asher said. "Ruby tells me the crowd this week was much larger, so I can't imagine next week."

"Izzy will love this. We'll definitely be here," Oliver replied.

"Thanks for the tour," Anna added.

"Of course. I also wanted to say how sorry I am," Asher said.

"Sorry? For what?" Oliver asked.

"For the torment my father put you through. For the deaths he's caused. I wish I could have stopped him, but I had no idea. I grew up thinking our family protected Briarwood, that we kept the people who lived there safe. I didn't know he and my sister were the reasons people were dying. He made the outside world sound so frightening, but he was the only one worthy of fear."

"You didn't know. He brainwashed you, and it's not your fault."

"Ignorance is no excuse."

"But you seem to be doing well. You've made a new life for yourself," Anna said.

"I fear I'll always be in his shadow," Asher replied.

Asher's words hit Oliver in the chest, and he spoke before he could stop himself. "Your father's dead, Asher. He passed away in prison."

Asher's eyes went glossy, and he looked down at his hands and avoided eye contact. "I've got to get back to the project," he said after a moment of silence.

"Don't you want to talk—"

"No, I think I've done enough talking for the day." He pulled open the door and gestured for them to leave.

"I'm sorry," Oliver said. "I know this isn't the best

way to find out, but it's important that you know. You don't have to worry about him or his shadow anymore."

Asher said nothing but made another gesture for them to leave.

"Why would you blurt it out like that?" Anna asked after Asher closed the door. "'Oh, by the way, your dad's dead.' Nice job."

"I couldn't help it. The guy's living in agony over what his father's done. I had to tell him."

They walked the streets back to Amberley station as Oliver replayed the events in his head.

"Don't be surprised if he never speaks to you again."

"We owed him the truth, don't you think? If I were in his situation, I'd want the truth." He hesitated. "You know, when my dad died, Mom waited a whole week to tell me."

Anna stopped walking and turned to face him. "What? That's awful."

"It was right at the start of exam week in college. She didn't want it to affect my scores and didn't tell me till I drove home for winter break. I came home on Saturday and had to go to his funeral on Sunday."

Anna found a bench near the station and pulled Oliver over.

"You never told me this."

Oliver stared off at the station, and Anna grabbed his hand.

"She was always so hard on the guy. Then all the stress was finally too much for him, and she hid it from me. *That* wasn't her decision to make. Having her in Christchurch just dredges everything back up. I know she thought she was doing what was best for me, but it really messed me up." His voice quivered.

"I'm sure."

"And to see Asher walking around, thinking his father's still alive. I know it's not the same, but..."

Oliver hadn't confronted these feelings before and didn't realize the weight he'd been carrying. Seeing Asher had pushed him over the edge.

Anna said nothing but sat with him on the bench until he'd regained composure.

CHAPTER SEVEN

No matter how hard he tried, Oliver couldn't rid the conversation with Anna from his mind. He tried to work up the courage to approach his mother several times, and finally, several days after their visit to The Parlor, he swallowed his nerves and broached the topic of his dad with his mom. Although their relationship was still jagged around the edges, both he and his mother had made efforts to bridge the rift that had existed between them for some time.

He asked her to join him out on the back porch. "I should have said this the other night after our roaring success of a welcome dinner." He leaned in close to her.

His mom chuckled. "Can't say it was the warmest welcome, but you apologized, and that's all that matters."

Oliver looked down at the table. "That's what I wanted to talk about. I *am* sorry for keeping the move from you, but I don't regret my decision to move here, and I'm not ashamed of it. I'm happier now than I've ever been. I have friends and family here, and I've learned a tremendous amount in the past year, helping Izzy with the bakery and the hives. I know how to take care of bees now. Bees! Remember how afraid of them I used to be?"

His mom paused for a moment. "You know I'll always love you, but I can't pretend that I approve of what you're doing. I just don't understand it."

"You don't have to understand. That's the best part about it. You don't have to accept it either. You just have to accept me."

She sat back in her chair and scowled. "For you to sit here and insinuate that I don't accept you—I can't believe it."

Oliver rubbed his temples hard. "If that's what you want to take away from this conversation, then there's not much I can do about it."

His mother pursed her lips.

"You judge," he blurted out.

"Excuse me?"

"It's what you do. I tell you the truth, and I feel like you judge me for it. Everything is a massive guilt trip with you. I feel like I'm a constant disappointment—

always have." He'd said too much too quickly, and the truth spewed from his mouth as if it were a leaky faucet.

"Well, I guess I'm just a terrible mother," she said in a matter-of-fact tone.

"See! You're doing it right now! I can't have a conversation with you that isn't passive-aggressive and guilt ridden."

"I am not being passive-aggressive," she said through gritted teeth.

"You treated Dad the same way."

The line seemed to catch her off guard.

"I know it's no excuse to lie to you, but I'm hard enough on myself without you piling on, and so I distanced myself, especially after what happened to Dad."

Her expression softened somewhat. "His death was hard on both of us, but that's hardly an excuse," she replied.

"Do you know how painful it was to find out Dad had been gone for a week and you hadn't bothered to tell me? I apologized to you for keeping Christchurch a secret, but you never apologized for keeping Dad's death from me. And my secret pales in comparison."

Oliver saw a little crack in his mom's tough exterior, and she wiped the corner of her eye.

"You know I thought I was doing what was best for you," she said. "You had to focus on school."

"Being home with my family would have been best, and it should have been my decision to make," he said, voice shaking.

His mom was quiet.

"Don't you have anything to say?" he asked.

"No," she replied. "You've made it clear how you feel. I need a little time to process." Her voice was low and reserved.

"Okay." He took a deep breath. "For what it's worth, I'm not trying to be harsh, but I realized I'd been holding on to so much anger. I thought I had let it go, but you being here is bringing everything rushing back."

She didn't come back with a passive-aggressive remark, which told him she'd listened, but he worried he had pushed the woman too hard.

After the conversation, his mom spent the next few days reading alone in her bedroom. He gave her space but wondered if she was truly mulling over their conversation or was simply angry with him.

On top of the strained relationship with Bev, Oliver worried about how he'd left things with Asher. The day of the next menagerie show arrived, and Izzy and Oliver climbed into the station wagon to go see the Amberley show and Asher's new exhibit. He assumed they were still invited but worried about the reception they would receive when they arrived.

Will Asher even want me to come? He imagined Ruby would be furious, although she didn't seem to have much of a penchant for anger.

Izzy's fingers wrapped around the steering wheel in an arthritic death grip. Oliver had planned to drive, but she insisted. She pulled the station wagon through the center of town.

"Nothing from your mom yet?" she asked.

"Not a word," he replied.

"I'm sure she needs time to think. The woman wouldn't have stayed *this* long if she wasn't giving serious consideration to the things you said. Do you feel better about it?"

"I feel much better now it's out in the open. I didn't realize I'd been carrying all of that resentment." He looked off into the distance as they passed the Christchurch sign.

"So what's in store for the Halloween menu this year?" he asked, trying to shift the conversation to a lighter topic.

The holiday was still several weeks away, but they started celebrating as soon as the first leaves changed colors in late September.

"The usual. We're also going to try bear claws with chocolate fur and fondant fingernails and

Cthulhu cupcakes." Izzy perked up in her seat as she answered.

"Cthulhu?"

"Think giant octopus god," she replied.

"Sounds promising."

"He's my favorite deity," she added.

Oliver had seen Izzy do little driving outside of the town square, and now he understood why. She'd driven the Christchurch streets a thousand times before, so her driving was automatic. As the road wound around the countryside to Amberley, she struggled to keep the station wagon on course. She'd veer the wheel every time she turned her head to talk to Oliver, and he had to warn her several times of upcoming bends when she became distracted by conversation.

As Izzy pulled the station wagon onto the main drag of Amberley, colorful decorations lining the streets greeted them. Orange and yellow streamers hung across the street lanterns, the lights of which were made to look like jack-o'-lanterns. Store owners had lined their windows with cobwebs and monsters of various shapes and sizes.

"These decorations blow Christchurch out of the water, don't they?" Oliver asked.

"I've never been here with Halloween decorations up. This is incredible!"

Izzy made the turn past the church and parked

across the street from The Parlor. A line extended out the door and wrapped around the sidewalk.

"Wow, word must be getting around," Oliver said.

"And this is all because of the guy from last year?" Izzy asked.

"Asher? Not entirely. You'll see once you meet Ruby. She has a few talents of her own."

Jen noticed the pair standing at the base of the steps and waved them toward the doorway.

Oliver and Izzy squeezed their way past the line and to the front door.

"Ruby's got chairs reserved for you. Go on in," she said.

"Crazy crowd tonight, huh?" Oliver asked.

Jen gave him a sarcastic eye roll. "You don't say."

"I feel like royalty," Izzy said, looking back at the line.

"Let's have a look around. You have to see the chandelier," Oliver replied.

As Izzy entered the lounge, her eyes shot upward toward the bone chandelier, and her mouth hung wide open.

"Crazy, isn't it?"

"This must have taken ages," she replied.

The bar distracted her as she turned toward Oliver. Caleb was, once again, pouring shots of the pear-colored liquid into funny-looking shot glasses.

"Absinthe!" Izzy pushed her way through the crowd and toward Caleb, who set a tray of the fancy glasses on the bar. Oliver tried to keep up, but the undulating crowd blocked his path.

The place must have been at least two or three times busier than the last weekend. After a few side steps, a twist, and a turn, he caught up with Izzy, who was already leaning against a small exposed area of the bar, clutching a small glass.

"Absinthe?" Oliver asked from behind.

"'After the first glass of absinthe, you see things as you wish they were. After the second, you see them as they are not. Finally, you see things as they really are, and that is the most horrible thing in the world.' At least, that's what Oscar Wilde said. Sounds fantastic, doesn't it?" After Izzy's monologue, the surrounding crowd seemed to second-guess whether to try the mystery drink.

"Don't worry, folks. It's pure bunk, I promise you. Hallucinations have always been a rumored side effect of the wormwood in absinthe, but it's only the alcohol that's responsible for any pink elephants you may encounter," Caleb said. "This small sample won't do any damage, but you can take an entire bottle home with you this evening for a mere $45. Be sure to smell first, then sip to clean the palate. Let the absinthe wash over your tongue."

Caleb noticed Oliver standing behind Izzy at the bar and reached across to pat him on the shoulder. "Oliver! Glad you could make it. Should be a great show tonight."

"This is Izzy, my gre—my aunt." He caught himself but still received a subtle jab from Izzy, who had already emptied her absinthe glass.

"A pleasure," Izzy added. "But it appears someone has forgotten to fill my cup." She winked at Caleb and held out her empty glass.

"I'm going to have to keep my eye on you," Caleb said, "but I think I have something you might enjoy even more."

He knelt down behind the bar and returned with a bottle and three fresh glasses. He leaned between Oliver and Izzy so that the other guests couldn't hear. "We save this for special occasions. This puts the stuff we serve to everyone else to shame. Three hundred bucks a bottle, so savor every sip." He poured a small amount of milky-white absinthe into each glass.

"Hold on a minute," he said as Izzy lifted her glass. "Always dilute it first, or else you'll be sorry in the morning." He pulled three odd-looking spoons and set them across each glass, then placed a sugar cube on each. As he poured water over each spoon, it gradually melted the cube and trickled through the slits underneath.

Once Caleb had finished preparing each glass, he raised his for a toast.

"To Asher and the two who saved him," Caleb said, tipping his glass toward Oliver.

"Hear, hear!" Izzy added.

Oliver laughed and took a sip. Based on the odd color, he expected an acrid taste, but the initial bitterness faded into pleasing herbal notes.

"Not too bad, right?" Caleb asked.

"Not what I expected," Oliver replied.

Someone across the hall distracted Caleb. Ruby stood halfway out her office door, frantically waving for him. He looked at his watch then slid the bottle back behind the bar. "Missed my cue. Head on in and take your seats. Time to get things started."

Oliver was relieved that Caleb had greeted him warmly, easing his fear that the man would show them the door.

As Izzy and Oliver passed Ruby's office, she tapped Izzy on the shoulder. "You must be Oliver's aunt. So glad to meet you. Saved two seats for you up front. Think you will like the new display. Asher's been working on it all week."

Caleb's voice boomed from the other room, encouraging the audience to take their seats in front of the stage. Izzy and Oliver sat in the seats Ruby had roped off at the front of the room.

The crowd shuffled through the rows of chairs. Once they had settled, Jen placed the needle on the record player, and the lights went dark. As they waited for the show to begin, Oliver heard the clinking of glass overheard.

When Ruby pulled the cover off the first aquarium, Izzy whispered, "Skeletons? What a cool trick. What are they swimming in?"

"You don't want to know," he whispered back. In telling the story about Briarwood to Izzy, Oliver had told her about Asher's blood, but she had never seen it for herself.

Izzy stared intently as Ruby traced the glass with her finger and several of the fish followed. When she tapped her knuckle on the glass, she sent the fish into a frenzy, and a few launched toward the source of the sound, collapsing like tiny accordions against the wall of the aquarium.

Midway through the show, Caleb brought the house lights up, and Oliver looked up at the ceiling.

He swore he heard something above them, but the can lights overhead seemed to be brighter than last time, and he found it hard to look at them for any length of time. There seemed to be some sort of rack underneath the light mounts, but he couldn't make out what it held.

Oliver watched Izzy's reaction closely when Ruby

pulled the cover off the mirror. Although he'd seen his emaciated reflection before, it still made him shudder, and one day, it wouldn't be an illusion. Izzy cupped her hand over her mouth in amazement at the image in front of her.

"Before you depart for the evening, I have something special to share with you—an addition to our collection of cadaverous creatures," Ruby said after snapping the reflection of the audience back to normal. "The person responsible for some undead wonders you see here tonight has been hiding behind the scenes, and since our new addition to the Grim Menagerie is so fantastic, we felt it only fair that the creator should be the one to unveil it. Asher, if you please."

Asher appeared through the side door to the stage and nervously paced toward the center while refusing to make eye contact with the crowd. He cleared his throat, and his voice wavered at first. "Thank you, Ruby. Fortunately, our new display needs no unveiling, since it's been hanging right above your heads this entire time." He gestured toward the ceiling.

Asher walked toward the back of the stage and unwound a rope from a stage hook. Metal squealed against metal as the mystery rack lowered from above the crowd.

A dozen or so specimen jars were suspended sideways from a makeshift frame made of plumbing pipes.

As they passed through the wall of light and into view, the can lights backlit the jars, casting a shifting red glow onto the crowd and revealing the creatures inside. Somehow, Asher had assembled a fleet of skeletal monkeys, which stared down at the crowd, pantomiming their way around the large jars.

"I hope you enjoy our undead troop," Ruby added, but the new display preoccupied the crowd.

Several stood to get a closer look, and Oliver laughed when Izzy let out an audible gasp next to him.

"What kind of voodoo is this?" Izzy asked.

Oliver looked back at the mirror and scanned the crowd to see their reactions through the reflection. As he looked at the back of the room, he noticed a man standing against the wall. Oliver recognized the dingy sweater and hunch of the man who had danced his way through the alley on Oliver's second visit to The Parlor. He seemed unaffected by the visual above him and instead slid out from the back row of chairs and started down the aisle toward the stage. Oliver thought perhaps the man was planning another impromptu dance session, but as he came closer to the mirror, Oliver noticed a flash of something metal in his hand.

When the man made it to the base of the stage, just a few steps from a nervous Asher, Oliver stood and shouted a warning over the commotion of the crowd. When Ruby made eye contact with him, Oliver pointed at the man in the aisle. She locked eyes with him and said nothing but pointed up at the ceiling. The man stopped and looked up at the display overhead. He let out a terrified scream as one of the heavy glass jars broke loose from the frame and crashed down upon him, sending blood, bones, and broken glass everywhere as it hit its target. The man fell out of Oliver's sight, behind a row of people.

Ruby stood in front of the man, glaring down at him. She whispered something to Asher, who quickly disappeared through the doorway on the side of the platform.

A few of the audience members moved in to help, but not before Caleb rushed to the aisle and picked up the knife, sliding it into his sleeve and concealing it from the crowd. He pulled the man to his feet and escorted him down the aisle and out of sight. The debris that had fallen on him had vanished, and the jar was now safely back in place in the metal frame.

"Isn't the first time we've had someone screaming on the floor, but I assure you, this time, it's all part of the show," Ruby said, scrambling for words.

The crowd laughed, and the cover-up seemed to work, although some still seemed confused by the vanishing glass.

"Thank you all for visiting the menagerie this evening. Please stay and have a look around. Our creatures don't bite as long as you keep your distance."

The crowd erupted into applause once again, and Ruby seemed to regain composure as she bowed.

"Did you see that?" Oliver asked.

"Yeah!" Izzy replied. "It looked like the jar broke off the display, didn't it?"

"No, the man had a knife, and it looked like he was coming after Asher."

"Knife? What are you talking about? She said it was all part of the show." Izzy marveled at the structure suspended above their heads. "What a great illusion."

"It's not an illusion," Oliver replied.

As soon as the audience dispersed, trickling around the room and back to the entryway to take in the obscure gallery of oddities, Oliver sidestepped the crowd and headed toward Ruby's office.

"Where are you going?" Izzy asked.

"Come with me," he replied. "I have to make sure they're okay."

"Who's okay?"

He ignored her question but pulled her toward the hallway. Light was creeping out under the office door, and Caleb greeted him when he knocked.

"What happened?" Oliver asked, eyeing Ruby, who was sprawled across a violet chaise in the corner of the room. Asher sat in a leather wingback chair behind Ruby's desk and shifted his eyes away when Oliver's met his.

"I told you this was a mistake." Caleb shot a glance at Ruby.

"Asher can't live in hiding forever. He's already spent the first quarter of his life in a cage," she replied from under a cold compress.

"But to put him on display like that?"

"His dad's dead. He's no longer in danger. Nice job letting me tell him, by the way." She shifted her sights to Oliver.

"Clearly, someone's still looking for him," Caleb replied.

"Fred's a loon, and the crowd probably overwhelmed him. He thinks we're all evil, anyway."

Izzy squeezed by Oliver and stepped through the doorway. "Would someone tell me what's going—"

She stopped short when she saw Asher behind the desk. The last time Izzy had seen him, he'd cowered behind the couch after she knocked Simon down the staircase. Although she'd had but a moment with the man, Oliver slowly filled her in on who he was and why he had been covered in his own blood.

"Anna and I saw that guy—Fred—digging in the trash when we came to visit after the show," Oliver said.

"Fred's usually harmless, or at least that's what we

thought. He goes around the neighborhood and picks the aluminum cans out of the trash. He's been acting strangely this week, just standing outside and trying to look through the window. He'd never hurt a fly, so I'm not sure what's gotten into him," Ruby said.

"What did you do with him?" Oliver asked.

"Threw him out back and locked the door," Caleb replied.

"What if he comes back? Did he say why he did it?"

"I'll handle it if he shows up again. Couldn't understand what he was saying half the time. Most of it was a load of gibberish, as usual. But he put up quite a fight for a man who can barely stand up straight and took a firm jab at my face." Caleb rubbed his upper lip. "I think he nearly knocked out one of my teeth. He seemed to calm down once I got him outside, and he even apologized. He said he'd been possessed. We'll have to be more careful with him around. I'm not one to call the police, but I will if I have to."

"He was trying to get me," Asher said. "He stared right at me as he came up the aisle. I stood there like some fool. Thankfully, Ruby was looking out for me."

Ruby lay down on the couch. "You can thank Oliver for that. If he hadn't shouted, I wouldn't have even noticed Fred."

Asher shrugged and refused to make eye contact with Oliver.

"You don't look well. Are you all right?" Oliver asked Ruby.

"I'll be fine. I hadn't planned for that final illusion." She winked. "I think the shows are catching up with me, and it feels like I've been hit by a freight train."

"So it wasn't real?" Izzy asked.

"'Real' is a relative term," Ruby replied.

"Do you think it's safe for Asher to stay here? Maybe he could come stay with us," he said. "If it's all right with Izzy. We've got plenty of room, don't we?" He normally wasn't one to volunteer someone else's house, but he knew Izzy wouldn't mind.

"Of course," she replied.

Asher didn't say anything, but his eyes darted to Caleb as if looking for assurance.

"He'll be fine here," Caleb said. "We'll just need to take some additional precautions, and he won't be making any future appearances at the menagerie shows." He shot a glance at Ruby, who responded with a smug smirk.

"At least take our phone number," Izzy said, "just in case. Our door is always open." She looked around for a scrap of paper.

Caleb tore a scrap from Ruby's desk ledger and handed it to Izzy with a pen.

Ruby sat up in the chaise. "Well, I have readings to do, and you ought to go out and make sure no one's robbing us blind," she said to Caleb.

"Jen's out there," he replied.

"You think Jen would hop up from that stool if she saw someone stealing? She's making minimum wage."

"Fair point. We should really give the girl a raise."

"We ought to go, then," Oliver said.

Ruby stood and approached Izzy. "It was a pleasure to meet you," she said, gripping Izzy's hand.

"You too," Izzy replied.

As everyone but Ruby left the room, Oliver chased after Asher as he headed to the kitchen. "I'm sorry for how I told you about your father. I shouldn't have blurted it out like that."

Asher turned to face him. His fists were clenched, but he couldn't seem to get the words out.

"My dad died a few years ago, and my family kept it from me until I came home. I thought I owed you the truth. I would have wanted someone to tell me right away." Oliver tried to read Asher's expression, which seemed to shift from anger to sadness.

Eventually, Asher turned and walked away, and Oliver stood alone in the crowd.

Izzy was waiting for Oliver outside, and he convinced her to allow him to drive the station wagon home. Although she'd been adamant about driving earlier, the way home was poorly lit, and even she admitted she could barely see past the tip of her nose at night.

"What did you think of the show?" Oliver asked, trying to rid his mind of his interaction with Asher.

"Wasn't what I expected," Izzy replied. "Asher seems well, though, except for the whole assassination attempt, I guess."

"I hope he's safe there. I can't believe he went through everything with Simon, just to be chased by someone else."

"Maybe it was a fluke. They said this Fred guy has a few screws loose," she said.

"He didn't *seem* dangerous, just a little odd," he said.

"I'm sure they'll keep an eye out for him," she replied.

Oliver pulled the station wagon down the dirt path to Izzy's. The house was dark except for a dim light coming from the living room. He parked the car under the porte cochere.

"Looks like Momma Bev is waiting up for you," Izzy said.

Oliver laughed. "Considering tonight's events, I guess weirder things have happened."

They entered the house and walked to the living

room. Bev was sitting in the reading chair, and Pan was lying next to her on the floor.

"Have a minute?" she asked Oliver.

"I'm going to get ready for bed." Izzy patted Oliver on the shoulder. "Thanks for the adventure tonight, kiddo. Come on, Pan."

The pup was conked out, and Izzy had to clap her hands to wake him. He shook himself off and followed her up the stairs.

Oliver sat on the couch. "It's been quite a night. I'm exhausted."

His mom ran her thumb over the cover of her paperback.

"You know, when you were little, we had a rough go for a while—financially, I mean. Your father's firm went out of business, and he took nearly a year to find a new job. We had savings—thank God—but my part-time income from the bank was the only money coming in. We had to skimp and scrape to make it last. We tried to hide it from you, although not very well, I have to admit. You came home from school one day and told me kids were making fun of you for your gym shoes. 'They're not like the ones the cool kids wear,' you said. I was heartbroken. I marched down to the store and bought a new pair of shoes that night. In retrospect, it wasn't the most responsible thing to do, but I hated seeing you made fun of for something that was our fault."

"I don't remember that," Oliver said. "You and Dad did the best you—"

Bev held up a hand. "It's okay. I'm not saying this for sympathy. I want you to understand why I've been so hard on you. The world can be a cruel place, and I thought, by being the critical one, I'd be able to protect you from it. I know what it's like to grow up with nothing and to be made fun of for it. I didn't want to see the same thing happen to you, and I wanted you to have a better life than your father and I. I've been sick all week, thinking about what you said. I didn't know I was doing so much harm. As for Dad, I had no excuse for waiting so long to tell you. I wish I could take it back. I was just so worried about you passing your exams."

Bev crossed the room and sat next to Oliver on the couch. She placed her hand on his leg. "I see how hard you work at the bakery and how much Izzy and Anna care about you. I can see why you want to stay here. That's your choice to make, and I respect it. You're a smart boy, and I have to trust that you're doing what's best for you."

Oliver placed his hand on hers. "I appreciate that."

"I want to be a bigger part of your life than I have

been, and I realized that I'm a big reason why that hasn't happened."

"I don't know what to say."

"You don't have to say anything. You've been very honest with me—more honest than you've ever been before. I didn't realize how much you were holding in, and I want you to know that you can always be open with me. I'll try to do a better job, if you promise to give me a chance."

"Of course, Mom."

"Now, if you don't mind, it's well past my bedtime. I just didn't want to go to sleep without talking to you first." She smiled and rose from the couch.

"Have a good night," he said, still shocked by the sudden apology.

Oliver sat for a moment as Bev climbed the stairs. The day had been emotionally exhausting, and the conversation felt too good to be true. Eventually, he wandered up to bed, and for the first night in a while, he fell asleep as soon as his head hit the pillow.

CHAPTER EIGHT

Several days passed without any additional incidents at The Parlor, and life in Christchurch plugged along better than usual. Oliver's time with his mom had been great since their chat, and he felt a weight gradually lifting from his shoulders as their relationship improved.

The phone rang while Izzy was standing over the kitchen sink, scrubbing a particularly difficult baking pan, and Oliver was drying dishes next to her.

"I got it." He picked up the phone, but the voice on the other end was garbled. "I can't hear you. You're going to have to speak up," he replied. "Must be a telemarketer," he told Izzy.

"Caleb's dead," a hoarse voice said on the other end.

"What? Ruby?"

"I don't know what happened. I heard Asher yelling and caught Caleb trying to drag him out of the house. When I tried to pull him away, Caleb tried to strangle me. Before I could do anything, Asher hit him on the side of the head with a fire poker. We can't wake him up."

"Did you call the police?"

"And say what? One sight of this place, and they'd haul us away for sure. We can't. Someone's after Asher. I don't know who or how, but they've tried to use Fred and Caleb to get to him. You should have seen Caleb's eyes. They were dead—vacant. We can't stay here. Does the offer for Asher to stay with you still stand?"

"Of course," Oliver replied. "You too."

"I'll be fine. He'll be safe with you while I sort this out. I have friends in Amberley who can steer me in the right direction, but it's too dangerous for Asher to come along right now until I know who's behind this."

"I'm so sorry, Ruby. Are you all right?"

"Don't ask stupid questions." Her wavering voice became cold and clinical. "We don't have time to waste. Pull around back when you get here. I'll open the fence."

Oliver hung up the phone as his heart raced in his chest.

"What happened?" Izzy had dropped the pan back into the sink and tried to listen in on the conversation.

"I have to go to Amberley. Something's happened at The Parlor."

"Wait, why?"

"Caleb's dead. Asher killed him in self-defense."

Izzy's eyes widened. "What about Asher and Ruby?"

"I think Ruby's in shock, but they're both okay. Asher may be staying with us after all."

"I'll go with you."

"No, you stay here with Mom. I'll slip out the back door. Don't tell her anything. She'll just get in the way."

"You can't go by yourself. What if it's dangerous?"

"Caleb's dead. He's hardly dangerous anymore. Besides, Asher will need a place to sleep when he gets here. What if you took care of that while I'm gone? I'm still not sure how I'll explain him to Mom, but you can think up a story for that too."

"All right, but at least call Anna and have her go with you, in case you run into any troublemakers."

"I can defend myself, and I'm not exactly heading into a war zone."

Though he was trying to comfort her, the worry on Izzy's face was a look he hadn't seen on her often, and it made him uncomfortable.

"Unless you want me to die of stress by the time

you get back, call her," she said. "And call me as soon as you're on your way back."

He pulled Izzy close and kissed her on the forehead. "I'll be fine—I promise." He picked up the phone and punched in Anna's number. "But if it will make you feel better, I'll ask her to come."

As the town slumbered, Oliver grabbed the keys to Izzy's station wagon and pointed the car toward Anna's cottage. He hoped bringing her along wasn't a terrible mistake.

Oliver pulled the car up in front of Anna's, and he saw her outline standing on the other side of the stained-glass window in the front of the house. She opened the door and walked toward the car, bundled up in a heavy coat. He'd been so shaken by the phone call he hadn't bothered to grab a coat, and his adrenaline was his only protection from the cold.

"Are they sure he's dead?" she asked as she opened the passenger door.

"I can only assume. Remember the guy we saw in the alley the other day?"

"Yeah, the short guy with gross toes and the knife?"

"They thought it was a fluke—that maybe he'd just finally lost his mind—but Caleb proves otherwise."

"But what would make Caleb attack Asher?"

"No idea. He seemed fine on Saturday, and *he* was the one who fended off Fred. Ruby said it looked like he was dead behind the eyes—like he may have been possessed."

"What are we going to do?" Anna asked.

"We're going to pick Asher up and bring him back to Izzy's for now. He can wait it out in Christchurch until we hear from Ruby."

"How is he going to wait it out? He killed a man, and someone's going to have to answer for that. And what if whoever's after him figures out he's living in Christchurch? What if some creep shows up on Izzy's doorstep with a knife?"

Oliver's stomach went queasy at the thought. "I don't know, but we can't leave him there. They're both sitting ducks in that house."

His brain was on autopilot as he sped along the back roads to Amberley.

"Do you think it could be Simon?" he asked.

"I don't see how. Simon is dead," Anna replied.

"I know, but who else would be after him and why? The show seems like a gimmick, and surely no one would walk away thinking Asher could bring back the dead. Aside from you, me, Izzy, and Ruby, no one else knows what he's capable of."

They arrived at The Parlor in record time, but as Oliver cautiously pulled the station wagon through the narrow alleyway, he clipped the side mirror on a large metal drum tucked beside the building.

"Izzy's going to kill me," he said as he drove toward the back of the building.

A tall wooden fence blocked the rear of The Parlor, obscuring it from view. Ruby emerged from the back doorway and pushed open the gate, leaving just enough room to pull the car through. Once inside the courtyard, he backed the car up to the kitchen door, and Ruby shut the gate behind him.

"Are you all right?" Oliver asked.

Ruby said nothing in reply, but her eyes were red and puffy. She turned toward the kitchen and walked inside, beckoning them to follow.

Asher was leaning against the kitchen counter, head in his hands.

"We have to be quick," Ruby said, "in case someone is watching."

"I'll clear out the back seat," Anna said.

"No," Ruby replied, "they'll see him sitting in the back. You have to hide him until you're home. Don't let him out of the house once he's there. No one can know he's staying with you."

"Does Simon have something to do with this?" Oliver blurted out the question.

Asher looked at him then at Ruby. "He's dead. How could he?"

"Fred wasn't himself," she said. "Someone else is pulling the strings. I don't know how or who, but someone was controlling them with some force I can't even comprehend. Caleb would never..." She snapped her fingers at Asher. "Get into the back of the station wagon."

The snap caught Asher's attention, but he seemed to be in shock, his face pale and emotionless.

Ruby grabbed him by the shoulders. "I know you're overwhelmed, but we have to move quickly." Her voice cracked, but she walked away before he could respond. "His bag is in the hallway," she told Oliver.

Oliver entered the hall and grabbed the small duffel bag sitting on the wooden floor by Ruby's office. As he looked up toward the front of the house, he noticed an arm protruding from the lounge and lying limp against the hallway carpet. He took a step down the hall but second-guessed his decision and forced himself to focus on the task at hand.

As Asher climbed into the back of the car, Ruby kissed him on one cheek before turning to Oliver.

"Are you going to be all right?" Oliver asked.

"Keep him away from this place. If you need me, come to this address, but not unless it's necessary." Ruby handed Oliver a small slip of paper with a street number scribbled in ink. "And keep him out of sight. I'll be fine." She opened the gate for the station wagon to pass through then shut it behind them.

Anna helped Asher cover himself with an old

tablecloth that had been crumpled up in the back corner of the trunk.

Oliver could see the end of the alley in front, leading to the street beyond. As he pulled the car past a row of metal trash cans, a figure suddenly emerged from behind a can and blocked the car's path. Fred stood unblinking in the headlights, staring into the car and brandishing a blunt metal object.

Oliver slammed his foot down on the brakes, causing Asher to roll into the back of the leather seat.

"Would you watch what you're doing up there?" he said.

Fred approached the car as Oliver and Anna sat frozen in fear.

"Go! Floor it!" Anna shouted.

"I can't just mow him over." He had flashbacks to the Witch bouncing off his window in the Christchurch field.

Fred refused to move out of the way, instead placing his hand on the car and tapping the hood to get their attention.

"I have to go out there, or else he's not going to move," Oliver said.

"Are you crazy? He'll kill you."

"I don't have a choice, do I? He's an old man, and I think I can outrun him." Oliver cracked open the door and squeezed into the alley, keeping the heavy metal between him and Fred. "What do you want?"

Fred's response was incoherent over the sound of the engine.

"Speak up."

Fred held out the metal object he'd been holding at his side. "Dropped this."

"Bring it." Oliver reached his hand out over the open car door.

"Oliver, don't," Anna said from inside the car.

"Just wait a minute," he replied out of the corner of his mouth.

Fred squeezed between the brick wall and hood of the station wagon and handed Oliver the broken piece of side mirror he'd snapped off in the alley.

Oliver turned the object over in his hands. "Why did you try to attack Asher the other night?"

Fred tapped the tips of his fingers together as he mulled over the question. "'Devil's Song,'" he replied.

"What about it?"

"Got stuck in my head." He pressed an index finger into his temple and twisted. "Beautiful, though," he added.

Oliver climbed back in the car and shut the door. Fred stood to the side, providing enough room to pull the station wagon through without hitting the old man.

"What did he want?" Anna asked.

He tossed the broken mirror into her lap. "Just wanted to give this back."

"Did he threaten you?"

"Not at all. I asked him why he tried to attack Asher, and he said something about a song stuck in his head."

"Maybe he's just a dangerous loon," Anna replied.

"Ruby said it herself—he wouldn't hurt a fly. He's not dangerous. Someone made him do it."

Oliver looked in the rearview mirror, and just before he turned the corner toward the edge of town, Fred stepped out from the alley and looked down the road toward them.

"He's standing back there in front of the alley," Oliver said.

"We can't just leave Ruby there. If she leaves, he'll be waiting for her."

"She said not to come back," Oliver replied. "I told you what she did to the poor guy during the show. I think she can handle herself."

Oliver kept an eye on the rearview mirror to ensure no one was following, although he still felt somewhat paranoid for doing so. One assailant was dead, and they'd left the other in the dust in the Amberley alley. Still, without a clear idea of who or what had caused Fred and Caleb to attack, the danger seemed to be all around them.

When they reached Izzy's house, after having dropped Anna off at her cottage, his mom was sitting in the living room, cradling a glass of wine and buried in a book. Nekko was lying next to her, hogging most of the couch.

"I was beginning to worry," she said, looking up from her novel. "And who do we have here?"

Asher stood awkwardly in the doorway.

"Just a friend," Oliver replied. "This is Asher."

She scanned Asher with a critical eye.

"You were supposed to call," Izzy said as she climbed down the staircase. She didn't wait for an apology before turning to Asher. "Are you all right?" She pressed her palm against his cheek. "What happened?"

"Think we've done enough storytelling for the evening," Oliver replied. "Can we wait until tomorrow?" He nodded in his mom's direction, trying to remind Izzy not to reveal any of the details of their adventure.

"I set up a sleeping bag in your room and laid some fresh blankets and towels out too," Izzy said.

As she turned, Asher cleared his throat. "Thank you," he said. "I'm sorry to darken your doorstep this evening."

Once they reached the third floor, Oliver grabbed a pair of sweatpants and an old college sweatshirt from his closet. "Here's something to change into that might be more comfortable."

Asher sat on the sleeping bag next to Oliver's bed.

"I don't mean to be rude, but I could use a minute, if you don't mind."

"Of course," Oliver replied. "I don't blame you. It must have been a hell of a day."

"If you only knew," Asher replied.

As Oliver descended the stairs, he heard Asher sobbing and debated whether to go back. *He asked for privacy.*

Izzy was sitting on the couch with Pan snuggled against her, and both were deeply entranced in a nature documentary.

"A little old for a sleepover, aren't you?" his mom asked.

Oliver ignored the question but took a seat on the couch next to Izzy.

By the time Oliver climbed the stairs to go to bed, Asher was fast asleep in the sleeping bag Izzy had laid out for him, with Nekko pressed tightly against his torso. Oliver carefully tiptoed around the two and into bed.

He couldn't comprehend how it must have felt for Asher—someone who'd found his place outside the claustrophobic walls of Simon's secret chamber—to have everything stripped away again in a single evening.

* * *

"AND WHAT DO you do for a living?" Bev asked Asher, who was in midchew of a blueberry muffin.

"Not sure exactly," he replied. "Ruby always called it 'performance art.'"

"Performance art?" Bev wrinkled her nose. "How does that pay the bills?"

"Pays them quite well, actually. We typically have a full house on the weekends. Between the absinthe tastings, psychic readings, and reanimated animal exhibits, we do all right."

Bev's mouth hung open as she struggled to come up with a response.

"Don't grill him, please." Oliver stood at the kitchen counter, stirring a spoonful of sugar into his coffee.

Oliver wasn't prepared to explain the mechanics of Asher's abilities to his mother and still didn't quite understand them himself. He had coached Asher to leave out the more colorful details about his life so far, although Asher slipped now and then.

"I think I have a right to know who's spending time with my son," she shot back defensively.

"Maybe when I was ten," Oliver replied.

"It's all right. I don't mind. Shall I tell her how I reanimate the dead?" Asher smiled.

Oliver shook his head.

"You will not make a fool of me," Bev said, rising from the table. "I'll be in my room." She stormed off and thumped up the stairs.

"That went well, don't you think?" Asher asked, returning to his muffin.

"Maybe fewer details next time," Oliver replied.

"Are you going to tell her?" he asked.

"'Yeah, Mom, Asher here can reanimate dead animals, and his blood has magical powers. We're hiding him here because some evil force is trying to kidnap him. Another splash of coffee?' Remember, Ruby and Caleb are different. Most people wouldn't be able to handle the whole Unnatural thing."

"Fair point. I'm sorry. I'm just so worried about Ruby."

"Don't apologize. I'm worried too. I wish there was more we could do to help her."

Izzy walked into the kitchen and pulled a mug from the cabinet. "Already making friends, are you?" she asked Asher. "Whatever you said to Bev seems to have put her in a mood."

"Just telling the truth," he replied.

Oliver was eager to change the subject. "I was

thinking of showing Asher the hives today. Thought it would be good if we both got some fresh air."

Asher clammed up. "Do you think it's safe for me to go outside? Ruby said not to."

"I'll grab the beekeeper mask from the garage, just in case. No one comes out this way. Izzy's house isn't exactly a popular town destination. A stroll through the hives might help get our minds off of last night."

Asher looked worried at the prospect of leaving the house.

"It will be fine," Oliver added. "Just trust me."

The air was crisp, and the cold weather had calmed the bees. Still, Oliver pulled two masks from the garage and two sets of white gloves, just in case.

Asher refused to step through the back door until the beekeeping gear was on and Oliver had verified the coast was clear.

As they walked toward the hives, Asher swatted at the few bees that buzzed by his mask.

"They can't hurt you," Oliver said. "Just let them be, and they'll leave you alone. Keep swatting at them, and you'll regret it."

"Easier said than done. I've read about killer bees."

"These are honeybees. Not exactly the same thing. They're much less aggressive. Plus, it's worth risking death for a taste of fresh honey." He grinned.

"I wouldn't know. I've never had it."

"What? You've never had honey before?"

Asher shook his head.

"Oh. Well, what better time than now?" Oliver pulled the lid off one of the taller hives.

Asher backed away. "What are you doing?"

"We're going to taste a little honey."

"You can just take it like that, can you?"

"They don't mind. The bees are docile."

Oliver grabbed the corner of one of the hive frames and pulled it out, careful not to squish any bees.

A year ago, the hives had terrified him. His mind worked in worst-case scenarios, and he envisioned himself bursting through the back door covered in bees. Now he knew this was an improbable fear, and a year of Izzy's hand-holding around the hives—sometimes literally—had slowly but surely built his confidence.

Oliver lightly brushed a few bees away from the comb and pulled a small pocketknife from his pants pocket. He flipped the small blade out and poked it through one of the honey cells before gingerly replacing the frame in the box.

"Here," he said, handing the knife to Asher.

Asher looked at the amber goo with suspicion.

"Taste it," Oliver said.

Asher stuck the knife under his mask and brought it to his lips.

"Not bad for something that comes from bee spit, is it?"

Asher quickly pulled the knife from his mouth.

"I thought you were an avid reader. Read nothing about bees?"

"No, not honeybees, but you're right—it's not bad."

Oliver replaced the cap to the hive.

"Will the bees survive the winter?" Asher asked.

"We'll wrap the hives to keep them warm. This winter is supposed to be brutal, but they'll be fine if the hives are prepared correctly."

Oliver noticed Asher looking out at the forest in the distance. "What do you see?" he asked.

Asher rubbed the gold chain around his neck as he looked toward Briarwood in the distance. "Smoke," he replied.

CHAPTER NINE

The night of The Horseman's music fundraiser arrived. Izzy and Oliver helped with setup earlier in the day, assembling and decorating a large makeshift stage next to the bar.

Anna stopped by after closing the bakery for the evening. She had shed her floured clothing, let her hair down from its tight ponytail, and even dabbed blush on her cheeks. "I'm going down to the pub to have a drink before the music starts. Anybody want to join?"

Izzy popped her head out from the kitchen doorway. "Who are you, and what have you done with Anna?" she asked once she noticed Anna's unusually primped appearance.

"Thought it would be nice to dress up for a change."

"I think she looks lovely," Bev chimed in from behind her paperback.

"Thanks, Bev," Anna replied. "So what do you say? Who's in?"

"I'll be in the studio, my dear." Izzy carried a cardboard box toward the staircase. "Have to strike while the inspirational iron is hot."

"You mean you're not going at all?"

"I paid my dues this morning. Now, it's time to paint!"

"Oliver, what about you?" She had a look of desperation in her eyes.

"Sounds great," he replied. Just like Asher, Oliver was nervously awaiting word from Ruby, and he was eager for a temporary reprieve from the stress of the agonizing unknown. The Briarwood smoke added another element of worry. Although Oliver couldn't see it, Asher had described a billowing plume that swirled above the hidden town.

"You should take Asher with you," Bev added. She must have thought he was some kind of hermit since he never left the house.

Oliver hated the thought of leaving Asher locked away in the house for another evening, but he never seemed to mind being left alone with a stack of books. He couldn't risk Asher meeting the townsfolk.

"What about you, Mom?" Oliver asked.

Bev seemed surprised. "Oh no, I couldn't. I'm not really a pub person, and I'm just getting to the good part of my novel."

"I have a feeling your novel will be here when you get back. Live a little."

Bev hesitated for a moment. "Okay."

Oliver was surprised by her answer. "Really?"

"I could use some fresh air. Been cooped up in this house for too long."

Anna turned toward him, her back facing Bev. "Wow," she mouthed.

Bev set her book down on the table.

While she went upstairs to change, Anna sat on the couch next to Oliver. "Things seem to be going well. Can't believe she's coming with us."

"She's lightened up," he replied. "We've got enough on our hands, with Asher's situation as it is, so I'm glad we've been able to make up."

"Speaking of, have you heard anything from Ruby?"

"Not a word. I'm sure she's all right—or at least I hope—but I'd sleep better if we heard from her." He looked down at his lap.

"You don't suppose we could try to find your mom a nice Christchurch beau, do you?" Anna did her best to lighten the mood.

"You might even find someone for yourself," he replied.

"Not exactly surrounded by eligible bachelors around here," she said.

"What about Tim McDonald? He seems nice."

"Tim McDonald used to lick the back of the bus seats in elementary school."

"So he's probably in need of a girlfriend, then," Oliver replied.

"Where is Asher?" she asked.

"Upstairs reading, I think. He can always help Izzy with her toe paintings if he gets bored."

Anna giggled.

"I'm serious. She's made a whole series."

Since he arrived, Asher had been making his way through Izzy's library, reading anything and everything he could get his hands on. He was already three quarters of the way through *1984*, which he'd started that morning.

Bev returned from her bedroom, purse tucked under her arm and ready to go. "Shall we?"

Oliver changed out of his pajamas as he mentally prepared himself for the night out at the pub with his mom. Fortunately, they'd be surrounded by a bar full of other people and loud pub music.

After he changed clothes, Oliver met Anna and Bev downstairs, and they took the dirt road to The

Horseman. The owners of the pub had fully decked it out in Halloween decorations, including cobwebs strewn over the windows and a large scarecrow posted in the center of the courtyard.

Although the show wasn't to start for another hour, the place was packed by the time they arrived. They squeezed by a large group of smokers who'd congregated around the entryway, trying to absorb the radiant heat from inside while they puffed.

Large carved jack-o'-lanterns sat on either end of the large wooden bar, and mummy wrappings hung from the top liquor shelf.

"Oliver, be a dear and order a glass of sauvignon blanc or something dry if they don't have it. No way I'll be able to squeeze through to the bar without being trampled. I'll find us a table." Bev strode off toward a vacant high-top table in the back corner of the room.

Oliver gave Anna a side-eye. "Are you too dainty to order your own drink too? Happy to bring you something."

Anna laughed. "Be nice to her. I'm very capable of ordering my own drink, thank you." She shoved her way through the crowd of minglers and up to the bar, leaving Oliver to follow in her wake.

"A stout, a lager, sauvignon blanc, and three shots, please," she said to the bartender, pointing at a bottle of local whiskey on the shelf.

"Planning on being carried out?" Oliver asked.

"A shot for me, you, and Bev," she said over her shoulder.

"No way we're getting Mom to do a shot." Oliver pulled out his wallet, but Anna resisted.

"This one's on me," she replied.

Anna handed Oliver a shot, and they clinked glasses and downed them before returning to their table.

"Your face is red," Bev said to Oliver. "You feeling all right?"

Anna giggled. "It's just a little warm in here," she lied.

Oliver put the shot glass and the glass of wine on the table and slid them over to his mom.

"Are you nuts?" she asked.

"Remember, we're living a little tonight, right?"

Bev lifted the shot glass and sniffed, snarling at the nose-burning odor.

"Do it," Oliver said.

Bev took a sip from the glass and choked the whiskey down.

The shot made small talk with his mother significantly easier. He even found it slightly pleasant. Whenever they'd wander onto an awkward topic, Anna would jump in to course correct.

The mayor served as the MC for the evening and had even borrowed a sequined suit for the occasion.

A hat was passed around the bar as the first group took the stage. Martin had coaxed Harry, whose wife was the first casualty of the last year's attacks, into playing guitar while Martin sang a few traditional Irish tunes. Although Martin was typically conservative in looks and demeanor, he came alive onstage. He strolled across the room and serenaded Madeline, whose cheeks were so red with embarrassment they nearly matched her cabernet.

"Izzy will wish she came when we tell her about this," Anna said.

"Maybe not," Oliver replied. "Eric's got a video camera over there. We may be able to get a copy of the tape for posterity."

Several others took to the stage that night, including a few Oliver had never met before. As the evening progressed, the crowd became more and more participatory.

Eventually, the night drew to a close, but before the mayor concluded the evening, he noted a late addition to the show's lineup.

Heads turned as the woman walked toward the stage.

Bev snickered. "You've got to be kidding me. Looks a little out of place, doesn't she?"

Oliver rolled his eyes and took another swig of beer.

The musician strolled across the stage, her tightly bound bleached-blond dreadlocks bouncing as she did. Her face shimmered in the spotlight, cheeks glittering with highlighter against pearly white skin—skin that seemed almost impossibly pale. Her coral eye shadow matched her vinyl jacket, offset against elbow-length leather gloves running underneath the sleeves.

Bev was right—the woman didn't fit in, but Oliver grew annoyed as several other snickers emerged from the crowd.

The musician pulled a stool in front of one microphone and set her violin case on the stage next to her. She seemed undeterred by the crowd's less-than-friendly welcome and tuned her violin.

"She realizes it's not Halloween, right?" Bev laughed.

"Would you knock it off?" Oliver said. He looked at Anna to provide reinforcements, but she was busy chatting with a man at the table next to them.

"What?" Bev replied. "Not my fault she's dressed like a slutty bride of Frankenstein."

Oliver finished the rest of his beer in a single swig, refueling himself with liquid courage. "Remember the talk we had about being critical of other people?" He set his glass on the table hard, catching Anna's attention.

"What happened?" she asked.

"I've upset him, apparently," Bev replied. "He's being a sissy, if you ask me." She grinned.

"All right. That's enough for me." Oliver stood up and turned toward the door, but Anna caught his arm before he escaped into the crisp fall night.

"Where the hell do you think you're going?" she asked.

"Home," he replied. "Can't deal with her anymore."

"What am I supposed to do?" she asked. "You can't just storm out and leave me with her. She had a few too many white wines, and the whiskey probably didn't help. Cut her some slack."

"Have yourself a girl's night, drink, get up onstage, and sing the National Anthem—I don't care—but you're going to do it without me." He pulled his arm away and was out the door before Anna could say another word.

He cooled off halfway through the walk home and felt guilty for leaving Anna alone with his mom. He had probably overreacted, but he couldn't turn back now. Although he might have been overdramatic, he would not apologize, especially after their earlier discussion.

Oliver noticed the back-porch light was on as he approached Izzy's house. Asher was sitting wrapped in a blanket and reading under the floodlight and perked up when he saw Oliver.

"Aren't you freezing?" Oliver asked.

"I'm sorry. I hope it's okay that I came out here. I needed a change of scenery. I hope you don't mind—I had to get out of the house." Asher seemed overly concerned.

"It's fine. No one will see you, but I'm shocked you came out on your own." Oliver pulled up a chair across from Asher.

"The music already wrapped up at the pub, then? Where is everyone else?"

"I came back early."

"Why?"

"Long story—started when I was born, actually."

Asher cocked his head. "Your mom?"

Oliver nodded.

"Want to talk about it?"

Oliver shook his head. "I'd rather just sit here for a while, if that's okay with you."

Asher nodded.

Oliver sat in silence for a few minutes while Asher flipped through a few pages of his book.

"It wasn't reasonable for me to expect her to

change overnight. I may have gotten through to her, but she's still got the same cynical bones," he said.

Asher set his book down. "I thought you didn't want to talk about it. What happened?"

Oliver smirked. "She made a few remarks and called me a sissy. I don't think she meant it, but she's said things like that before, and it always gets under my skin." He felt silly saying it out loud.

On one particular occasion, he'd come home from college for the weekend with a new haircut—one he was particularly fond of. "It's a tad feminine, don't you think? Don't want people to think you're—you know..." she had said, flipping her wrists forward. He went back to the barber the next day and came home with a buzz cut.

"If it makes you feel better, my father used to drink my blood," Asher said casually and cracked a smile. "I've been told that's not a normal thing for fathers to do."

"That puts things into perspective."

"I've been having nightmares about him and Briarwood," Asher said. "It's so strange that the town's just across the field. I can see the smoke rising over the trees."

"I can take you to the edge. We could get a closer look," Oliver replied.

Asher bristled. "I don't know. Nothing good waits for me there."

"You're safe as long as you don't cross the patch. No one can get to you without that key around your neck."

Asher looked down at the table. "Perhaps it's an adventure for another evening."

Oliver planned to stay out until his mom returned home, but after an hour of sitting outside with Asher, the warm fog of beer and whiskey had worn off, leaving him with no shield from the cold, aside from a light jacket.

"I'm going to bed," he said, standing up from the patio chair. "Don't stay out here too long, or else you'll get sick."

"I don't get sick," Asher replied. "One perk of magical blood, I guess."

"Lucky you."

Oliver walked through the kitchen and into the living room to find Nekko. After a thorough search, he found the chubby tabby under the couch. She'd pulled an entire loaf of bread off the counter and was chewing through the plastic in a fit of hungry kitty rage. He'd forgotten to feed her before he went off to the show.

Oliver returned to the kitchen to fill Nekko's bowl then carried it and the cat up to his room. While she munched loudly on the windowsill, he replayed the night's events in his head while lying in bed.

Eventually, he dozed off before his mom wandered her way home.

Oliver awoke in the middle of the night when the creaking floorboard and hallway light pulled him from sleep. He assumed it was Asher coming to bed, but he rolled over and saw his curly brown hair peeking out from underneath the blanket draped across the sleeping bag. Oliver checked the clock—3:00 a.m. As he pulled the sheet over his head to shield his eyes from the bright light, he noticed a pair of feet standing on the other side of the doorway.

Is Izzy sleepwalking again?

He waited a few moments, and eventually the person on the other side of the door turned around and entered the bedroom across the hall.

CHAPTER TEN

The alarm clock pulled Oliver from a delirious sleep—the kind of deep sleep that starts in a dream and ends in a state of temporary amnesia. As his momentary confusion faded, he turned off the alarm, and Asher shuffled in the sleeping bag on the floor next to him.

Oliver rubbed his forehead and cleared the sleep from his eyes before forcing himself to abandon the warm cocoon he'd created under the covers and flinging his limp legs over the side of the bed.

No matter how many times he woke up for his early shifts at the bakery, he'd yet to become a morning person. After he climbed over Asher, he looked back at him and felt a hint of jealousy creeping up his chest.

Izzy had left a while before but was kind enough to leave a half pot of coffee piping hot in the Butler.

Oliver huddled around his warm cup and relived the last night's events. Now that he had a few hours of sleep under his belt, his mom's transgressions seemed less severe, and he wondered if Anna had been right—maybe the wine had gotten to her head.

Izzy had taken the station wagon to work, so he was forced to march the cold path to the bakery. Mist had settled in over the square, and all Oliver could see of the statue of Samuel Hale was a hand gripping a large cross peeking out over the crest of the fog.

The bakery sat like an island in the middle of a sea of gray. As he entered the front of the store, Oliver heard a flurry of pans in the kitchen. He turned the corner to see Izzy standing over a dropped muffin tray, cursing at the oozing batter slowly creeping across the tile floor like a B-movie creature.

Izzy looked up at Oliver with a glare that said "Don't you dare ask me if everything's all right."

"Where's Anna?" he asked instead.

"She no-showed on me. We've been working together for years, and she's never just blown off work."

"Did you call her?"

"You bet I did. Said she wasn't feeling well. I took that as she was too hungover to come in. I like a glass of honey wine as much as the next, but that's no excuse for missing a morning bake."

"I have to admit I'm feeling a little groggy this morning too."

"So you were her enabler!" Izzy pointed a rolling pin in Oliver's direction.

"Hardly. I ended up leaving early."

"Well, Bev must have had fun, at least. Didn't hear her come in until three in the morning."

"So that *was* her creepily standing outside my door."

"Maybe she had trouble figuring out which bedroom was hers. The woman can put away some white wine," Izzy said. "Give me a hand with this, would you? I've got to finish frosting a birthday cake and need to ice the pentagram cookies."

"Pentagram cookies? Don't you think they might be a little risqué for Christchurch?"

"They're for Halloween, and I would never have any fun without some risk of controversy."

Oliver knelt down and scooped the muffin batter back into the tin before tossing the whole thing into the sink. "Why didn't you call me earlier? I could have helped."

"I thought I could manage. Apparently, I was incorrect," she replied as she pulled a pair of hot trays from the oven. "Once you're done with opening the front, help me fill the display cases."

After cleaning up the mess on the floor, Oliver

started the coffeepots and ensured the front of the store was ready for customers. Although he felt bad leaving Asher alone with his mom, he enjoyed his time at the bakery over the last week, decorating the place for Halloween and finishing up the holiday mural.

He had decided against caricatures in favor of a haunted house. A large mansion sat atop a steep hill on the other side of a tall wrought-iron gate, highlighted by a bright yellow moon sitting behind it. He had dotted the eerie landscape with bright orange jack-o'-lanterns—one each for Izzy, Anna, and himself. He'd even created one for his mom, although its expression was slightly sourer than the others.

Oliver rushed around, frantically sliding Halloween-themed treats into the display cases. The furry bear claws turned out nice, although the Cthulhu cupcakes still needed work, since they looked more like a collection of snakes than giant octopus gods. Anna was typically the one to do the more advanced designs, but Izzy was trying her best, given the situation. Aside from the new treats, Izzy brought back a few favorites: pumpkin pielettes, brain brownies, and Frankenstein petit fours.

Izzy and Oliver prepped all the baked goods and filled most of the outstanding orders by the time the bakery opened. Oliver flipped the door sign to Open, then he and Izzy sat at the large metal table in the kitchen and had celebratory cups of coffee—a necessity if they were to last the day.

Although the cases were especially full and the coffee was piping hot, the bakery sat empty for the first few hours of the morning. Usually, the place was packed on Sundays as the Christchurch townsfolk took leisurely walks around town and stopped in for a bite to eat and coffee.

Just as Oliver was growing bored with staring out into the empty storefront, the bell jingled against the front door. Martin entered and slid into a booth.

"Hell of a night last night, wasn't it?" Martin asked.

"Sure was. The rest of the town must have had a long night too. We're usually swamped this time of day." Oliver said, flipping over Martin's cup to fill it with coffee.

"I didn't see a soul on my walk over here aside from a dog walker or two. Granted, most everything is closed on Sundays. Maybe it's the fog."

"Or the long night at the bar."

"Between you and me," Martin leaned in closer, "Madeline couldn't even leave the house this morning. She's still in bed. I've never seen her with a hangover before. I promised to bring her a cup of coffee and one of those pumpkin-pie donuts. I'll take a donut for myself too."

"Be right back with that," Oliver said, walking

behind the counter to fill Martin's order. "How did you like that girl with the violin?"

"She was phenomenal, at least according to Madeline. She had the whole place mesmerized, and you could have heard a pin drop, apparently."

"Really? Surprised to hear that. She didn't exactly receive a warm welcome. You didn't stay to hear her play?"

Martin pulled his right hand from his coat pocket and held it up for Oliver to see. His wrist was wrapped in a compression bandage.

"How did you manage that? Rock out a little too hard onstage?" Oliver asked.

"Ha! That would have been a better story. No, I tripped walking into the bathroom at the pub and twisted it trying to catch myself on the sink. It'll be fine, but it was throbbing so badly I went home early to wrap it. Kind of killed my social spirit for the evening."

"Well, hopefully the performance helped raise a lot of money. I can't wait to hear the totals."

Oliver set the bag of donuts and to-go coffee on the table, and Martin pulled out his wallet to pay.

Madeline must be off her diet.

"Keep the change," he said as he handed Oliver a bill.

"Thanks, Martin. Give Madeline my best."

Martin swigged the rest of his coffee and headed toward the door.

"Seems like Madeline had too good of a time last night too," he said, returning to the kitchen.

Izzy was busy rolling fondant over a cake she'd shaped to look like a miniature dragon. She'd crafted a modeling-chocolate birthday hat to go along with it too. "I must have missed out on all the fun. Sounds like quite the event."

"Me too. I'm not sure what happened after I left."

"I've had my fair share of nights I don't remember. Everybody needs to let loose now and then, even stodgy people like Madeline. It sounds like everyone let the night get away from them." Izzy carefully pressed the fondant around the cake.

"I guess so. Did Bev say anything to you when she came in last night?"

"Not a word."

Oliver returned to the front of the store and looked out the window into the mist.

The lull in business continued. Izzy used the time to get a head start on orders, and Oliver deep cleaned the booths. By early afternoon, they had completed every menial task they could think of, from scrubbing the kitchen to refilling the napkin holders.

"Let's close 'er up early today," Izzy said as she took another look into the empty storefront.

"You're the boss," he replied. He flipped the Open sign to Closed while Izzy turned off all the lights.

Oliver pulled his coat tighter around himself as he climbed into Izzy's car. They drove by the market, which was shut tight. The lights were off, and the sandwich board, which typically boasted its best deals, had been pulled inside.

The house lay quiet when Izzy and Oliver returned, and Izzy headed to the studio to paint. Bev lay sprawled on the couch, her paperback lying on the floor next to her. She was in the middle of a deep slumber and let out a dainty snore that reminded Oliver of the sound a bread knife makes as it saws across a crusty loaf. He crossed the room to the kitchen to pour a glass of water. He heard the scurry of Pan's feet across the deck and stepped outside to see what was causing the pup's excitement. Asher drew his arm back and tossed the tennis ball to the other side of the yard. Pan scampered after it, feet moving faster than his tiny frame could handle.

"Your mom's been sleeping on the couch all afternoon."

"She's never been one to nap. Did she say anything about last night?"

"No, but she's not very talkative around me. We mostly just sit in awkward silence. I'm used to silence, though. I don't mind it." He cocked his arm again as Pan waited eagerly.

"Did you notice her standing on the other side of the door last night? Creepy, don't you think?"

"Hardly. I slept straight through the night." Asher knelt as Pan returned with the ball, but the pup refused to let it go. "Guess we're done playing, then." He stood as Pan looked up at him with his head tilted to one side, still clinging to the slobbery ball.

When Oliver returned to the living room, Bev was sitting on the couch, flipping through her book and trying to find her place.

"How are you feeling?" Oliver asked.

"Just fine, Oliver. Why do you ask?" she replied coldly.

"I've never seen you nap in the middle of the day. You were drooling." Though she hadn't been, he knew she'd hated it when his father drooled.

Bev wiped the corner of her mouth. "We were out late, and I'm not as young as I used to be." She looked up at him and forced a smile, deep circles underlining her eyes. "Just need to fix myself a cup of coffee, and I'll be right as rain."

He assumed she hadn't forgotten about their little tiff, but Oliver wasn't going to be the one to bring it up. He turned toward the staircase.

"The young woman from yesterday is playing

again this evening. She was wonderful, wasn't she?" Bev asked.

"At The Horseman? I thought they were only doing music for the fundraiser. And what woman?"

"With the pretty dreadlocks."

Oliver turned. "Are we talking about the same person you snickered at last night? Surprised you were so fond of her."

"I did no such thing. I could never make fun of someone who's *that* talented. You heard her—what did you think?"

"I left early, remember?"

Bev seemed legitimately surprised.

"Oh, I thought you were there. Anyway, everyone was raving about her after the show. I spoke with Anna this morning, and we're going to the pub again tonight. Want to join?"

"Anna? She called in sick today."

"She must be feeling better. She sounded fine on the phone. Just a little tired is all. Go with us, won't you?"

Skipping out on work wasn't like Anna, and Oliver assumed only violent illness could have kept her away from the bakery. He was surprised she'd been so eager and willing to make plans, especially plans with Bev. *And since when did Anna and Mom talk on the phone?*

"I think I'll pass," he replied.

"Oh, come on. We'll have fun like last night."

Oliver gritted his teeth. *Last night wasn't fun.*

The thought of spending another evening with his mom made his head pound. "I'm going to stay in with Asher tonight."

"Bring him with you. About time he met people outside of the house, don't you think? He's such a hermit."

"He's a recovering alcoholic, actually," Oliver lied. "Pubs make him uncomfortable," he added, trying to put a kibosh on the conversation.

Bev seemed disappointed by the news.

"All right, then. I see some of us can't appreciate a musical genius when they hear one."

"Musical genius? Yesterday you were making fun of her. 'Slutty' was the word, I think. I'm surprised to hear you're so fond of her now."

"Oh, I was just joking. I would never make fun of someone for their looks."

Oliver held in a chuckle.

"I guess Anna and I will be the ones to have all the fun," she said.

Pan burst into the living room, still clenching the ball tightly in a corgi death grip.

"He doesn't understand how fetch is supposed to work." Asher came in and took a seat in the reading chair across the room.

The doorbell rang as Bev was tying her shoes.

"That'll be Anna," she said.

"She never rings the bell. Isn't she going to come in?" Oliver asked. He walked down the hallway to the front door.

"No, I'll get it," Bev said from behind, nearly tripping over her shoelaces, but Oliver had already opened the door.

Anna had deep bags under her eyes, and her hair looked as if she'd just rolled out of bed, strawberry blonde strands clumped to one side of her head.

"You look like hell," Oliver said.

"Glad to see you too," she replied.

"What's the deal? You never called in."

"I had a rough evening last night and felt like my head was going to explode this morning."

"And now you're headed down to the pub? Better not let Izzy find out."

"I'm not Izzy's slave. I can do whatever I please," she said with an edge in her voice.

"What's gotten into you?"

Bev pushed by Oliver. "Let's be off," she said.

Anna glared at Oliver for a moment then turned around and plodded down the stairs with Bev but without so much as a goodbye.

"She was in a bad mood," Asher said as Oliver headed back to the living room.

Anna's reaction was making Oliver's blood boil. "I can't believe she blew Izzy off and now she's going to the pub."

"The pub? Again?"

Oliver shrugged.

"Why didn't you go with them?"

"Thought I'd hang out here with you. Hardly seems fair to make you stay here by yourself all the time. And also, can't say that I care to be around either of them at the moment."

"I'm perfectly capable of entertaining myself, you know," Asher replied.

"I know."

"I appreciate the sentiment, though," Asher added. "The house has been dull lately. I finished most of the interesting books, and soon I'll have nothing to do but sit and worry about Ruby."

"I know," he replied. "I'm worried about her too."

After an early dinner, Oliver and Asher hung around the house while Izzy painted in the studio.

Oliver sat on the couch with Nekko asleep in his lap. Her belly fat hung over the sides of his legs, and he finally became so overheated he had to move her. "Come on, let's go for a walk."

"Walk? Where to? What if someone sees me?"

"Everyone will be down at the pub, by the sounds

of it. We're going in the opposite direction. I think it's time we go to the edge of Briarwood."

Asher hesitated. "I can't."

"You said it yourself: you wanted to know what happened to the place. Let's go find out. We don't have to go in. We'll just have a peek."

"What if someone in Briarwood sees me?"

"No one will see you—I promise. And even if someone on the other side of the patch notices you, there's nothing they can do to hurt you."

Oliver could hear the commotion from the pub in the distance as they stepped out onto the back porch. The entire town must have been there once again.

With flashlights in hand, they trekked down the grassy hill to the overgrown field sitting next to Briarwood. The last time Oliver had ventured down the hill, he came barreling back in a police cruiser, killing the Witch and arriving just in time to reach Izzy before Simon did. He'd had no reason to return to the field nor the briar patch where he'd found Lilly Brighton's body more than a year before. Without the Briarwood key, the woods were just an ordinary clump of trees, and the secrets held within them were beyond his reach.

As they reached the patch under the cloak of darkness, Asher froze, staring into the woods ahead.

"What's wrong?" Oliver asked.

"This was a mistake," Asher replied.

"Why?"

Asher turned toward him. "I should have never let you talk me into this." His face was pale, and he backed away from the woods.

"I just thought it's what you wanted—to find out what happened to the town. I didn't mean to upset you."

"It's horrible." Asher's eyes shot briefly to the woods before flashing back to Oliver.

"Let me see." Oliver held out his hand.

Asher took his hand, breaking the invisible barrier camouflaging the town.

The stone two-story that had tipped Oliver off to the town's existence lay in ruins in front of him. The line of streetlamps had been bent and toppled, leaving no lights to show the way into town. He couldn't see much beyond the ruined structure, but a plume of smoke in the distance was a sure sign that things had not been going well in the town hidden beyond the trees.

"You see? Look by the doorway."

As Oliver looked closer at a pile of rubble by the broken doorframe, he noticed a body slumped over against the crumbled stone—a woman, he thought, but it was hard to tell through the layer of soot and ash.

"I'm sorry. I didn't know." Oliver pulled his hand

away as a knot formed in his stomach, and the scene vanished.

Asher turned and marched up the hill. "I'm going back."

"Wait for me!" Oliver rushed to catch up with him.

Asher's eyes glistened with tears.

"I'm sorry. I was stupid to bring you here. I don't know what I was thinking. Let's just go home and forget about it. We never have to come back."

"I can't go home," Asher replied, twisting around to face him. "*Home* doesn't exist anymore. My *home* has likely been burned to the ground," he gestured toward the tree line. "My *family* is dead—my father, Caleb, and probably Ruby."

"You don't know Ruby's dead. I know what's happened to you is terrible, but—"

"I'm leaving," Asher interrupted.

"What? You can't leave. Where will you go? Someone's chasing you."

"And you don't think they'll find me here? If someone truly wants to track me down, wouldn't it make sense to come to Christchurch? Wouldn't it make sense to come to the only other place with which I have a history?"

Oliver could think of nothing to say. He and Asher stood face to face, consumed by the silence of the chilly fall night. Finally, Asher turned and resumed his march up the hill toward Izzy's house.

Oliver barely recognized the man, who was clenching his fists in anger. He differed from the meek boy who Simon had dragged to the house a year before, cowering in the corner while his father tried to dispatch one last Elder. For a moment, Asher had shed his submissive shell.

Oliver reached the house shortly after Asher, although he tried to maintain his distance. They'd been gone for an hour or so, between the walk to and from the woods, and Izzy appeared to have already gone to bed, since her studio light was off.

CHAPTER ELEVEN

Oliver entered the house and turned the corner from the kitchen into the living room.

Asher was standing in the center of the room. "Your mother nearly gave me a heart attack," he said.

The house was dark, except for the floor lamp over Bev's chair, casting an eerie shadow down her face.

"Everything okay?" Oliver asked.

The corners of her lips curled into a smile. "My, you were out late," she replied.

Oliver looked at his watch. "It's only ten."

"I've been waiting for you two."

"Waiting up for me, are you? You know I'm not in high school anymore, right?" He laughed.

Bev, however, sat in silence. Then she stood up and walked toward Asher, and the light from the lamp caught the edge of a chef's knife she'd pulled from between her thigh and the chair cushion.

"What are you doing?" Oliver asked.

"We're all going to take a walk to the studio."

Asher backed away from Bev toward the front door.

Oliver's heart dropped as he thought of Fred walking up the aisle at The Parlor show, knife in hand.

"Put the knife down, Mom."

"She told us about a boy who looks just like you," Bev said, flicking the knife in Asher's direction.

"She?" Oliver asked.

"Said you'd taken something that doesn't belong to you—that you'd probably shown up a few days ago. As soon as she said it, I knew it had to be you."

"Mom, where's Izzy?"

His mom cackled in a way he'd never heard before. "Dumb broad didn't even see it coming."

Oliver turned toward Asher. "Go get help."

Asher reached for the door handle.

"No, no. Let's take a trip up to Isabelle's studio," Bev said. "She promised to play a special song for the person who finds you. That's me!" She clapped her hands together in excitement, the handle of the knife dampening the sound. "I never win anything."

Oliver crossed the room and stood between her and Asher. "We're not going anywhere until—"

"You've always been useless. Just like your father," she blurted, her expression shifting from glee to contempt. "No ambition—can't keep a job. What did I do to deserve you?"

The question sucked the air from Oliver's lungs. "I—"

"I said go up the goddamned staircase!" she screamed, lunging forward at him and pressing the edge of the blade against his side. Bev's face came close enough for him to see her vacant eyes.

"I won't say it again," she added in a singsong voice.

Asher pulled his hand away from the door and approached her. "It's okay. If it's me you want, then let Oliver go. I'll come with you."

Bev rolled her eyes. "Enough with the sappy spiel. Get moving." She prodded them up the staircase and to the door of Izzy's studio. She pulled a skeleton key from her pocket, unlatched the door, and forced them inside. She locked them in then plodded down to the first floor.

In the dark, Izzy's paintings loomed over them, the caricatures even further exaggerated by the moonlight.

Oliver searched the wall for a light switch and flipped it on. Behind him, Asher gasped, and Oliver turned to see Izzy standing in the center of the room.

"Oh, thank God!" Oliver said. "Why were you standing in the dark?"

"The darkness calms me," she replied. "Calms Pan too." She pointed at the dog bed in the corner, where Pan lay curled up in a corgi ball, fast asleep.

"How long have you been in here?"

"An hour or two. I don't really know. I was up here painting, and Bev must have come back from the pub early. I heard her come in and thought she was coming up to say hello—wishful thinking, I guess. She locked the door, and I've been up here ever since. I tried shouting for her, and I know she can hear me, but she's just been ignoring me. What's gotten into her?"

"It's the same thing that happened to Caleb and the homeless man, Fred. They both tried to take Asher." Oliver thought for a moment. "Fred pretended to play the violin and said a song got stuck in his head. It has to be the violin player who came to the pub. Somehow, she's controlling them."

"Why not just take me, then? Caleb tried to drag me through the door and out onto the street. Why bother locking us up here?" Asher asked.

Oliver walked to the far window overlooking the front porch. "I don't know, but we shouldn't stay to find out. We could hop out onto the porch roof. The drop to the ground isn't that far."

"Who do you think I am?" Izzy looked out onto the ground below. "I can barely go up and down the steps without falling. Might as well ask me to somersault across the room."

"We can help you," Oliver said.

"I'll just slow you down. You two go, and I'll stay here," Izzy replied.

"We can't leave you," Oliver said. "What about Mom? What if she comes up here and sees we're gone? Who's she going to take her anger out on?"

"I think I'll be able to handle her. Remember when I knocked that old kook down the stairs last year? Sorry, Asher," she added. Then she walked to the corner of the room and pulled a bat from behind a set of metal shelves. "I have another haymaker right here. I'd be more worried for your mother if I were you."

"How many of those do you have hidden around the house?"

"Let's see: one in my bedroom, one by the front and back doors, another out in the shed—"

"Sorry I asked," he replied.

Oliver and Asher quietly opened the window and slipped out onto the porch roof, shoes sliding on the shingles.

"We'll come back for you," Oliver said.

"Don't worry about me." Izzy pressed a palm to Oliver's cheek. "I'll be fine."

Oliver hung off the edge of the roof and stepped

down onto the porch railing. Once safely on the ground, he guided Asher down.

"We'll take the car," Oliver whispered. As he rested his hand on the metal latch, he realized the keys were somewhere inside, where Bev was waiting in the shadows.

The wind had picked up since their journey to the edge of the woods, and although the town was quiet, the sound of rustling leaves made him feel as if they were being watched, surrounded by unseen foes standing just beyond the reach of the streetlamps.

"Where are we going?" Asher asked.

"To the police station. They'll be able to help us."

They passed the pub, which was oddly dead for that time of night. The lights had been turned off, and Oliver couldn't see a soul nearby. The town was the same, and the streets were dark and empty.

As Oliver and Asher approached the station, he had flashbacks of the night Simon had slammed into the town statue, when the station had been filled to the brim with officers from neighboring towns. He hadn't been back since, although he'd bumped into Eric, the Christchurch chief of police, now and then at the bakery or out at the pub.

The pub.

"I'm so stupid," Oliver whispered.

"Why?"

"Eric was at the pub last night. He'd be under the same spell as Bev. We can't go to the police."

"Who does that leave then, if the whole town is affected?" Asher asked.

Oliver looked across the square at Fletcher Antiquities. Martin's car sat out front, and although the sign was flipped to Closed, the back-office light was on.

"Martin. He missed the show. Maybe he can help us. If we can just get his car, I've got Ruby's address."

They crossed the square and knocked frantically on Martin's door. Martin had nodded off at the desk in the back of the office, and the knocking startled him awake.

"What are you doing out at this time of night? And who's your friend?" he asked as they rushed inside.

When Martin pushed the door closed, Oliver locked the dead bolt.

"What's gotten into you?" Martin asked.

"Did you go to the show tonight?" Oliver asked.

"I've been here doing inventory. What's the matter?"

"Mom's gone crazy. She locked us all in the studio and was walking around with a chef's knife. I think it's the woman—the one who played the violin the other night. She's been hypnotizing people and probably has most of the town under her spell at this point—Madeline too."

Martin backed away. "Have you been drinking?"

"I'm not drunk. We have to take your car and get help before they hurt Izzy or us if we stay here for too long."

"Have you lost your mind?"

Oliver grabbed Martin by the arm and tried to put together a sentence that didn't sound insane. "Mom has Izzy locked in her studio, and she's running around with a knife. She's not in her right mind, and we need help."

"Have a seat, and I'll give Eric a call," Martin replied.

"No, you can't! We have to leave town. Eric may be in on it too."

Martin hesitated. "Let me grab my things. If this is some sort of practical joke..."

They followed him to the back of the store, where he pulled his coat from the rack and opened one of the desk drawers to grab his car keys.

A knock at the front door startled them all.

Eric was standing close to the glass and knocked again as he peered inside.

"Maybe we should ask Eric himself?" Martin said.

"Don't let him in," Oliver said.

However, Martin was already halfway up the aisle to the door. Oliver followed, with Asher close behind, and tried to step between him and the door, but Martin shoved him aside.

"What's gotten into you?" he asked as he unlatched the door. "Eric, what the hell is going on?"

Eric seemed calm at first glance, and for a moment, Oliver wondered if he too had been spared. But then he looked at Asher, and his eyebrows flinched. "Sorry to bother you, Martin, but Oliver's friend here is in a whole heap of trouble. He'll need to come with me."

Asher looked at Oliver but didn't budge.

"He's not going anywhere until you explain," Oliver said.

"He needs to come with me now. We'll take care of him," Eric replied.

He stepped toward Asher, but Oliver stepped between them.

Eric locked eyes with Oliver and cocked his head slightly. "Very well," he said and took a step back. As Oliver turned to face Asher, Eric cocked his arm and slammed his fist into Oliver's cheek, sending him tumbling into the side of a heavy wardrobe.

Martin stood frozen, seemingly unsure of whom to trust at the moment.

Asher shouted as Eric grabbed him by the collar and pulled him through the door and into the darkness.

As Oliver pushed himself up to his feet, still reeling from the blow, he stumbled toward the door.

He couldn't see anything beyond the front door—the night was too dark—but he noticed a light switch next to the doorframe and flipped it on. The outside shop lights illuminated the edges of the square, and to Oliver's horror, a group of townspeople had encircled the front door. They stood in silence, arms at their sides and only swaying slightly in the heavy breeze.

Eric handed Asher over to several others then turned back toward the storefront, while Martin stepped outside. Oliver didn't wait to see what happened next but turned and sprinted to the back room of the store. He knew Martin's shop had a back courtyard and only hoped the townspeople hadn't surrounded the building.

He unlatched the heavy metal door to the courtyard and nearly lost his balance and fell as he scaled the wooden privacy fence. At first, he heard shouts from behind, but darkness shrouded the edge of town, and Oliver quickly slipped away into the side streets. He felt sick to his stomach for having left Asher behind, but he'd be of no help if the townsfolk captured him too. He wasn't sure where to go—the town seemed to have lost its collective mind.

He headed in the direction of the train station, working his way around the perimeter of the square and sneaking in from the back. The station was eerily quiet. Although the last train had already come through for the evening, the station gate was ajar.

Oliver sat on a bench under the dim lamplight in the empty station and took a moment to catch his breath. He felt truly and utterly alone. Izzy and Asher had been captured, and Anna wasn't herself anymore. Clearly, they wanted Asher, but Oliver could only hope they wouldn't dispose of Izzy once he'd been captured. If they had wanted to kill anyone, though, Bev surely would have done it earlier that evening. She'd chosen to lock them all up instead.

What do I do now?

He pulled his wallet from his back pocket and shuffled past a few bills and pulled out the small slip of paper Ruby had given him. The address was in Amberley, but no phone number was listed, and he had no way to get there.

He spotted a pay phone at the far end of the station and felt a glimmer of hope as he held his breath and reached into the phone-book cubby. In the city, mysterious substances covered what few pay phones still existed, and all the phone books had been either stolen or destroyed. This was Christchurch, however, so he pulled out a crisp phone book.

The taxi promised to arrive in ten minutes or so, but ten minutes came and went as Oliver waited conspicuously in the station. He debated whether to take his chances on the dark road out of town. He was a sitting duck in the station, and surely someone from the town would wander up in this direction if he waited too long.

Then Oliver saw headlights coming down the road, and the knot in the pit of his stomach dissipated. He approached the yellow cab and climbed into the back seat.

CHAPTER TWELVE

Oliver held his breath around the twists and turns leading to Amberley. As the taxi's headlights illuminated the darkness smothering each curve, Oliver expected the mob to greet him.

The taxi driver pulled down a narrow street and parked in front of an old apartment complex.

"Sure this is the place?" Oliver asked.

"This is the address you gave me," the driver replied. "Cash or charge, bud?"

Oliver pulled out his wallet and slipped the driver two crisp bills. A fine mist fell from the sky, causing the complex's cement stairs to glisten as Oliver hurried to the front door. He pulled on the handle, but the entrance was locked tight.

A buzzer system hung on the wall next to him.

Ruby had only given him the address and hadn't bothered to tell him the room number.

This can't be right.

Oliver descended the front steps and stood in front of the building once more, mist slowly seeping through his jacket's fabric. Somehow, he'd missed a small set of stairs nestled under the main entrance. He followed them down to a sturdy black door, gripping a wrought-iron handrail as he approached. He tried to peer inside, but the small diamond window in the door had been covered.

He pulled the door open and had to duck through the doorway to avoid hitting his head. The ceilings were low and lined with faded copper paneling. The place was styled like an Irish pub, but it lacked the jovial atmosphere. In stereotypical fashion, a bartender stood against a backlit bar, drying a glass with a towel.

"Help you?" he asked, looking out over the glasses resting on the tip of his nose.

"I'm looking for Ruby," Oliver replied.

The statement caught the attention of a stringy-haired man sitting in the corner of the bar. He looked over at the bartender then back down at his half-empty pint.

"Name?" the bartender asked.

"Oliver."

He set the glass down and reached underneath the

bar. "Broom closet next to the men's room. And don't forget to hit the switch when you're on the other side."

Oliver furrowed his brow but thanked the man and followed the hallway to the restrooms. He pulled open the door to the broom closet to look inside. The broom closet was typical, with a mop and bucket and several shelves of cleaning supplies. However, this broom closet had no back. A dark hallway sat on the other side, lined with paneling and dimly lit by flickering wall sconces.

When he stepped through the back of the closet and into the hallway beyond, he found the switch on the wall and pressed it as the bartender had asked. The missing wall shot up in front of him, sealing him inside the mysterious hallway. He walked cautiously toward a doorway at the end of the hall and heard chatter coming from around the corner. He found himself in another bar, much like the one he'd just been through, except this one was full of people.

Oliver received several stares as he crossed the bar and approached the bartender. The man was identical to the one he'd just met on the other side of the wall.

Twins? "I'm looking for Ruby," he said.

The bartender didn't respond with words but rather nodded to his left.

Ruby sat tucked into a booth along the far wall. It was raised from the floor slightly and hidden within a wood-paneled cubby. She was in deep conversation with a man across the table, leaning in so as not to be overheard. When she saw Oliver, she did a double take, and a look of panic washed over her face. As he approached, she signaled for the other man to leave, and he slid out of the booth, nodding at Oliver as he returned to his friends across the room.

"What are you doing here?" Ruby asked. "Is Asher all right?"

"They've taken him," Oliver replied.

"Shit," she said under her breath as she rubbed her temples. "Have a seat."

"We have to go back to Christchurch. He's in danger."

"It won't do much good without a plan. Drink?" she asked, tilting her glass in his direction.

"Not sure this is a good time—"

Before he could finish, Ruby snapped her fingers, grabbing the attention of the bartender. She held up two fingers, and he nodded then turned to the taps behind him.

"Trust me. We're not going anywhere tonight," she said.

"But they've taken him. The whole town has gone mad. Izzy's locked up in the house, and my mother pulled a kitchen knife on me. How can you be so calm about this?"

Ruby looked up at Oliver, her bloodshot eyes meeting his. "Make no mistake—I am not calm. I am hanging by a thread. But panic will get us nowhere. If they've taken the town, we need a plan. I should have known they would find him. I was foolish for sending him to stay with you."

The bartender set two frosted pint glasses in front of them. "Who's your friend?" he asked.

"This is Oliver," she replied, "the one I've been telling you about."

"Oh. Pleased to meet you." He extended his hand, which Oliver shook. "Drink's on the house, then. Enjoy." The bartender pulled a rag from his back pocket and crossed the room to clear a dirty table.

"On the house?" Oliver asked.

"You're a celebrity around here," Ruby replied.

"A celebrity? For what?"

"For saving Asher last year. I've been digging, trying to find out who's behind the attacks. When people heard what you did for him... Well, it's rare someone of your... normalness would do something like that for one of us. Word always seems to travel fast among the Unnaturals."

"So what is this place, then?"

"What does it look like? A reprieve from the oppressive world we live in. Everyone in this place is an Unnatural of some sort, except for you, I guess. It's why I came. I have friends here who can help."

"What about that guy?" Oliver pointed at the bartender.

"Charlie? Seems like he was in two places at once, doesn't it? Front bar and back bar?"

"I thought he seemed familiar. Just figured he was a twin."

"Ha! Lord help us if there were two of him. No, he can be in two places at once. Tried three places once but managed to split himself in half, and he took nearly a week to find his second set of legs. Still, he saves the owner a ton on labor costs."

"So what did you find? It's the woman with the violin, isn't it?"

Ruby nodded and leaned in close, holding her fist closed as if the secret were pressed into her palm. Oliver leaned in, and she opened her hand with a dramatic flourish, revealing nothing.

"Squat," she said. "No one's seen a thing. Sure, a few know Fred, but that's about it." Her eyes watered. "It's exasperating."

Oliver perked up. "I've seen her. She played her violin at the music night in Christchurch. Thank God I didn't stay for the performance, but I can at least give you a description. She's got dreadlocks, tattoos, and really pale skin. It's the violin playing, I think. It's like she hypnotized everyone."

Ruby took another swig of her drink and seemed to mull over the description.

"So what do we do now? Should we ask around?"

"How old was she?"

"I don't know. Maybe in her twenties."

Ruby wiped the corners of her eyes. "She doesn't sound familiar, but I may know someone who can help."

Oliver stood from the booth. "What are we waiting for, then? Let's go."

"Charlie, two black coffees." Ruby gestured for the bartender. "Told you I'm in no state to save the world tonight. I'm sure she's fast asleep, anyway."

"But what about Izzy? We can't just leave her. What if they try to hurt her?"

"If what you're saying is true, it makes no sense to kill someone when you can flip their will. I'll have Charlie set you up with a room tonight, and we'll leave first thing—" Ruby looked at her watch. "Er, second thing in the morning."

Charlie led them down a narrow hallway with skinny doors on either side. The scene reminded Oliver of the rooms at The Horseman, if he'd been looking at the hallway through a fun-house mirror.

"You lucked out," Charlie said. "This is our last free room, and it's one of the nicest."

He pulled a key from his pocket and slid it into the latch. For a moment, Oliver swore the room was as narrow as the doorway, with a cot nearly touching both walls and its headboard bumped up against a large metal water heater.

"Spacious," he said, trying to make light of the situation.

Charlie shot a sarcastic glance at Ruby. He pushed Oliver aside and twisted the water heater's pressure dial. The whole body of the water heater twisted around, revealing a door that had been cut out of the metal on the other side.

"We take security seriously around here," Charlie said. "Some influential Unnaturals have stayed in this very room."

"I'll be across the hall," Ruby said. "Expect a knock tomorrow morning." She grabbed Oliver's arm as he turned toward his room. "Because of you, we've got a shot at figuring this thing out."

Oliver stepped through the small portal in the water heater and pressed a switch inside the metal tube. The cylinder spun around faster than he'd expected, revealing a large room on the other side. He stepped through the cutout, and heat from a roaring fire hit the right side of his body. The room was two or three times the size of his bedroom at home. Portraits hung over the headboard of a four-poster bed, and a velvet sofa sat in front of the fireplace.

He picked up a business card from a stack on the table next to the entryway. Marv's Unnatural Bar was spelled out in gold letters. Oliver slid the card into his pocket and plopped down on the velvet couch in front of the fireplace.

His head spun as he tried to process the events of the day. Over the course of twenty-four hours, an entire town had turned on him, and Izzy and Asher had been taken. He hoped Ruby was right, that this violinist—whoever she was—would stay put and wouldn't harm Izzy. Asher still had the coin that cleared the way to Briarwood. If the woman discovered it and forced him to cross over, the odds were good that Oliver would never see him again.

CHAPTER THIRTEEN

Oliver awoke at a knock on the door. He'd fallen asleep on the couch with his face pressed against the soft velvet, and a pool of drool had collected at the side of his mouth.

The fire was still burning brightly, although he'd done nothing to keep the flame alive.

He stepped inside the water heater and pressed the switch, this time bracing himself for the sudden spin to the other side.

"Took you long enough," Ruby said. "Might want to fix your hair. Looks like you've just gotten out of bed."

"Off the couch, actually," Oliver said.

Ruby had transformed overnight. Her bloodshot eyes were bright and cheery, and she'd replaced the smudged eyeliner with crisp new wings. Her wavy hair bounced against the shoulders of her black sweater, the sleeves of which covered up the tattoos she typically showed off so freely.

"Looks like you're taking me to meet your parents," he said.

"Close enough," she replied. "Haven't seen her for a while and don't want her to think my life is in complete shambles."

After a quick breakfast at the bar, the two headed out for the mysterious destination and climbed the staircase up to the street.

"Okay to walk? It's not too far away," she said.

Oliver nodded.

As they walked, Oliver asked a question that had been lingering in his head for some time. "I've been thinking about this Unnatural thing. Asher has the key that clears the way to Briarwood. How does the key work? No one's creating an illusion. The power seems bound to the object itself."

"Magic left behind," she replied.

"What?"

"Most Unnaturals can leave pieces of themselves behind. It's expensive if you pay someone to do it for you."

"You mean people pay for it?"

"Leave too many pieces of yourself behind, and

soon there's nothing left to leave. Ought to cost a pretty penny, don't you think?"

"So someone must have made the key."

"Perhaps one of Simon's ancestors."

They came to a church, which Oliver immediately recognized as the same one that had led Anna and him to The Parlor.

"Thought we'd make a pit stop and check up on the place," she said.

The wrought-iron gate in front hung open, creaking in the breeze.

"You locked up before you left, didn't you?" Oliver asked.

"I did. Why?"

"Look." He pointed at the front door, which also sat open with a large gash between the door latch and frame.

They walked up the front steps, and Oliver carefully pushed the door open. The place had been ransacked. The large bone chandelier lay in shambles on the floor, femurs and rib bones scattered across the first floor as if the creation had exploded. Displays and bookshelves had been toppled and pictures ripped from the walls.

Ruby knelt in the entryway and picked up a busted picture frame. The image inside appeared to be a historic picture of The Parlor, taken when the streets were still dirt, capturing a horse midstride.

"The Parlor used to be a brothel, you know," Ruby said. "That little historical sidenote drew us in."

She looked at the dividing line between the entryway and the lounge, where Caleb had fallen, never to rise again. Oliver wondered what Ruby had done with the body but dared not ask.

"Took us years to restore the place. Someone had turned it into a damned hookah bar. Nearly had to rebuild all the woodwork ourselves."

"Do you think kids could have done this?" he asked.

She let out a heavy sigh and tossed the broken frame aside. Her heels pounded the hardwood as she paced down the hallway toward the stage at the back of the building, and Oliver followed closely behind.

The room looked like the scene of a murder. Sloppy trails of blood had been splattered across the floor, and bloody palm prints streaked the wall at the back of the stage. The large fish tank had been shattered along with the giant mirror, covering the platform in fish bones, broken glass, and puddles of blood.

"Not kids." She examined a clumsy set of footprints next to the base of the broken tank.

"Simon?" Oliver said.

"What?"

"Looks like someone climbed out of the tank. Look at the handprint streaks on the wall."

"But Simon's dead," Ruby replied.

"If he knew Asher's blood could be used to heal, perhaps he thought it could be used to bring himself back."

"But, Oliver, he's dead. How could a corpse have walked in here and climbed into a fish tank?"

"What if he's linked to the violinist? What if she's working for him?"

"Working for a dead man? How could he have orchestrated all this from beyond the grave? And even if Simon somehow made it into the tank—"

"He wouldn't be able to leave it, at least for long. Would he?" Oliver added.

"I don't see how."

"The bastards have taken the other tank too," Ruby said.

Oliver hadn't noticed, but the tank containing the undead birds was gone. He looked up at the ceiling. Someone had taken the rows of skeletal primate jars also.

"Come on, let's go," Ruby said, turning toward the front of the house. "Just need to make a call first."

She walked across the trashed hallway to her office, and Oliver followed closely behind. Papers had been scattered across the floor, and her heels dug into them as she walked toward the purple chaise. With one angry motion, she flipped it over and unzipped a zipper on the underside. She reached in and pulled out a small black address book.

"Thank God," she said. She set the book on the desk and flipped through its aged pages. Eventually, she reached the M section and ran a finger down a tattered page.

Ruby kept an old rotary phone on her desk. Many years had passed since Oliver heard the sound of a finger dragging around the circular dial and the whirring of the wheel spinning back to zero.

"Feel awful for not visiting her for so long. Hope she's doing all right," Ruby said.

The phone rang several times on the other end before a feeble voice echoed through the receiver.

"Marie?" Ruby asked.

"I know, I'm sorry. We've been so busy."

"Well, I was thinking of stopping by today, actually... if that's all right with you."

"Great! See you soon."

Ruby hung up. "Better be on our way."

The two left through the front door, and Ruby clicked the lock on the door handle and gingerly pulled the door closed.

"Not much protection, but hopefully it'll keep

anyone else from snooping around and causing any more damage," she said.

"I'm so sorry, Ruby," Oliver said.

"Me too."

As they left The Parlor and walked farther away from the bar, the scenery changed drastically. The historic brick buildings bled into boarded-up businesses and used-auto lots. They eventually arrived at a small subdivision. Rusted chain-link fences lined the broken concrete sidewalks, serving as poor barriers between passersby and the muscly fang-toothed canines that protected the properties.

They turned a corner and walked down another row of dilapidated one-floor houses sitting on concrete slabs, artifacts from the 1950s cookie-cutter-housing boom. Most had fallen into disrepair. The original siding had faded over time, and many of the decorative shutters sat crooked or were missing altogether. Broken-down cars sat tarped in cracked asphalt driveways, and even the squirrels seemed to be rougher around the edges.

Midway down the street, Ruby stopped and turned toward one of the houses. The owner had taken care of it even though this was the bad part of Amberley. Freshly painted baby-blue trim accented the bright-white walls, and the grass of the small lawn was a vibrant green and freshly cut and edged. Underneath a large bay window sat a bed of pansies that hadn't died with the first frost of the season, surprisingly. The place was an oasis in a desert of litter and dust.

A TV was blaring on the other side of the wall, and Ruby pressed the doorbell.

The front door cracked open, and a man's face appeared behind the screen door. His skin was streaked with brown swirls and patched with white. *Vitiligo*, Oliver thought as he, already over six feet tall, looked up at the man.

"Can I help you?" he asked.

"We're here to see Madam Marie," Ruby replied.

"Is she expecting you?"

"I called earlier. You'll find my picture on the wall next to the radiator. I'm an old friend," she said with a smile.

The man disappeared for a moment then returned to the doorway.

"She's napping now, but if you'd like to sit for a moment, I'm sure she'd be happy to see you." His serious expression had completely melted, and he grinned widely as he opened the screen door.

As they stepped inside, a faint whiff of mothballs filled the air, accented by the subtle scent of lilac.

"I'm Mo." The man wore a pair of light-blue scrubs and was made of solid muscle.

"Her nurse?" Oliver asked.

The man chuckled. "A nurse, yes, but mostly just a friend. I check on her in the mornings before my shifts at the hospital."

"Marie has lots of friends," Ruby said. "She's a well-connected woman."

"To say the least," Mo added.

Oliver and Ruby sat on an old olive couch covered with a multicolored crocheted blanket.

"She's been under the weather lately," Mo said. "Caught a cold and can't seem to shake it."

"How do you know Madam Marie?" Oliver asked, still waiting for someone to explain exactly who the woman was.

"She's saved us all at one point or another," Mo said.

"Saved you?"

Mo looked at Ruby. "Does he know about—"

She nodded. "He knows."

Mo's shut his eyes, and his fingers twitched on the arm of the chair. Then his head disappeared, followed by his arms. Mo was now a floating pair of scrubs hovering in midair.

"It was hard enough for my mother to deal with the fact I didn't look like everyone else. Found me like this while I was sleeping one morning, and that was enough for her. She took me straight to church—thought I was possessed. When church didn't work, she kicked me out."

Pale patches emerged from the sleeves of his shirt, and his skin gradually filled back in until it returned to its original mix of white and brown.

"How did you find Madam Marie?" Oliver asked.

"She found me. I had no money, so I broke into houses, which is easy to do when no one can see you."

"How did she find you?"

"Picked the wrong house one night. Even though no one can see me, dogs can still smell me. A Rottweiler cornered me in a closet. Nothing like a vicious beast to make you second-guess your life of crime. Fortunately, I'd wandered into a house that was friendly to people like me. The guy grabbed me by the collar and dropped me off at Madam Marie's. Said she'd helped him out and she could do the same for me. It was pure luck. Wouldn't be here today if it wasn't for her."

"What about you, Ruby?" Oliver asked. "How did you find this place?"

Ruby shuffled uncomfortably in her chair.

"Mo!" someone shouted from the other room.

"Sounds like she's awake," he said. "I'll take you to her."

He led them to a dimly lit room at the back of the house.

A woman sat slumped in an old armchair, her lap covered by a hand-stitched quilt. The smell of mentholated ointment filled Oliver's nose. Pictures lined the walls of the room, covering nearly every square inch of space.

"Oh! Ruby, so nice to see you, my dear!" Marie straightened in her chair as much as her hunched frame could manage.

"Oliver, this is Madam Marie."

"Nice to meet you." Marie extended a wrinkled hand, which Oliver lightly gripped. Her skin resembled cracked tree bark.

"My, my. How nice of you to bring such a strapping young man to my doorstep." Marie gave them a toothy grin. "Come sit." She tapped the edge of the bed next to her chair then turned toward them as they sat across from her. "What brings you to visit?"

Ruby leaned in. "Unfortunately, nothing good. We were hoping you could help us. Oliver's town is in trouble, and we think it has something to do with a woman —a violinist who seems to have hypnotized the entire town. She's made her way around Amberley, too, and we were hoping you knew something about her." Ruby left out the details about Caleb's death.

Madam Marie thought for a moment and turned to Mo. "You told me about a young lady who played the violin," she said.

"She had dreadlocks, didn't she?" Mo asked from the doorway.

"Right. You've seen her?" Ruby asked.

"I ran into a girl in the Amberley square. I knew when I saw her she was unique."

"You mean that she was an Unnatural?" Oliver asked.

Marie squinted at Oliver through her thick glasses. "I hate that word. *Unnatural*. What's natural, anyway?"

"It's not every day you see grown men throwing their wallets into violin cases of a street performer. She nearly pulled me in as well," Mo said.

"What did you do?"

"She had a bandage on her arm, and it looked infected. I brought medicine on my way home from work, and we struck up an odd friendship. Refused to tell me her name, so I just called her Siren. She liked it. She told me she was destined for bigger and better things and was waiting for a new job to pan out—something in the little town down the road. One day, I crossed through town on the way home, and she was gone. I haven't seen her since."

"If she's behind the chaos in Christchurch, how do we stop her?" Oliver asked. "How do we break the trance?"

"I can't help you with that, but maybe Marie can,"

he said. Mo looked at his watch. "I better be going, or else I'll be late for my shift. Just be sure to click the handle on the door when you leave. And make sure she takes the pills in the cup on the table." He pointed. "Have a good day, Marie."

"All right, sweetie. You, too, and stay out of trouble."

Mo nodded to Ruby and Oliver and headed toward the front door.

Marie thought for a moment. "I may have an idea. I knew a little girl, Minnie Rutledge. Came home from school one day, and her parents noticed she wouldn't eat. Asked her why, but she refused to tell them. They sent her to a doctor after a few days. After her parents prodding her, she admitted she wasn't eating because all her food was full of worms. Can you believe it? Prodded a little more, and she admitted she and a friend stole a candy bar from a shop on the way home. Her friend ran away, but the shop owner caught Minnie, yelled at her, and told her she wouldn't eat again until her friend brought the candy back."

"Seems a little severe," Ruby said.

"The candy bar had long been in the belly of Minnie's friend, so she had nothing to take back to him. They had to get poor Minnie a feeding tube. On one of their trips back from the doctor, a bad storm caused their carriage to run off the road. Everyone survived, but the shock seemed to have shaken Minnie right out of whatever trance that man had put her in."

"So what are you saying? A car crash is the only way to pull them out of it?" Oliver asked.

"Just a horse-and-buggy crash." Marie smiled. "A shock or scare should break the trance's hold. It worked for Minnie, and it should work for your friends. Maybe something as simple as a slap, unless it's a powerful trance. And the longer someone's in it, I imagine the harder it will be to pull them out."

Oliver was unsure of how he'd be able to shock the entire own out of hypnosis. Slapping them one by one, while fun in theory, would be impractical.

"Wait, horse and buggy?" he asked. "So you must have heard the story from someone else."

"No, I was there. Saw it with my own two eyes. Nannied for the family, actually."

"I'm sorry, but how could you have been there? That must have been the early nineteen hundreds if you were still using a horse and buggy."

"May 11, 1885, to be exact. Even made the newspaper."

Oliver didn't know how to respond.

"Madam Marie has her own unique ability," Ruby said.

Marie chuckled. "I guess you could say that. I'm afraid to say it's rather boring, though. Nothing like

Ruby here. You know, when she'd get mad at me, she used to make the pictures on the wall talk. She thought it would scare me, but I enjoyed chatting with all my old friends again."

Ruby blushed.

"Anyway, I expect this will not come as a shock to you, but I am ancient. I guess you could say that's my gift—or a curse, depending on how you look at it."

"I wouldn't guess you were a day over thirty," Oliver replied, straight-faced.

Marie chuckled.

"We should be on our way," Ruby said.

Oliver glanced at the photos on the walls as they prepared to leave. Some were newer and in color, while others were black and white on yellowing photo paper. The closer he looked, the more he noticed the same woman in all of them: Madam Marie. Although the pictures must have spanned nearly a century, Marie's appearance had changed quite slowly.

Madam Marie grabbed Ruby by an arm. "Good luck to you. Don't be afraid to call if you need help. I may not be able to do much, but I know people who can. Don't be so long next time. Can't promise I'll be able to wait for you."

Ruby kissed Marie on the forehead, and as she turned to leave, Marie called after her.

"And say hello to Caleb for me. Hope he's doing all right."

The words stopped Ruby in her tracks, and she had to compose herself before speaking. "I will" was all she managed to say.

"How did you meet Madam Marie?" Oliver asked once they had reached the sidewalk and headed back toward town.

"She found me heaving in an alley in Amberley," Ruby replied.

"What do you mean?"

"My parents gave me an early Christmas present one year: a packed bag and a swift kick out the front door. My story's not so different from Mo's, actually."

"Your parents just kicked you out?"

"I may have made a turkey dance across the table at Thanksgiving. I wasn't exactly the nicest teenager, and that was the last straw for them. The timing was poor because the weather was so cold. I tried to sleep out on the streets but got horribly sick."

"How did she know about Caleb?" he asked.

"Caleb grew up across the street, the yellow house back there. The place didn't look like it does now. This street used to be one of the nicest in the neighborhood. He asked me to marry him twice in that house. The first time, I said no. Didn't think he'd handle all of this

Unnatural business well. But he kept at it and refused to take *no* for an answer."

Oliver didn't know what to say, so he put his hand on Ruby's shoulder and squeezed.

After a few moments, Ruby wiped the corner of her eye. "So we need a shock," she said.

"Fred. He seemed perfectly normal when we ran into him in the alley, the night Caleb... You must have snapped him out of it when he tried to attack Asher. Think you could do the same for an entire town?"

"I can try. That would take a much larger illusion, though." Ruby seemed hesitant. "Either way, sounds like it's time we pay Christchurch another visit."

CHAPTER FOURTEEN

B ack at Marv's Unnatural Bar, Ruby pulled a stool up to the bar. "Take a seat," she told Oliver.

"A little early in the day, don't you think?" he replied.

Ruby rolled her eyes. "We're not here for the booze. We're here for Charlie."

The name must have caught the bartender's ears because Charlie appeared from behind the bar as if he had risen through the floorboards.

"Here for an afternoon pick-me-up?" he asked.

"We need a car," Ruby said.

He looked behind the bar and rifled through a row of glassware. "Fresh out of those," he replied with a smug smile.

"What about the big guy? You think Marv's got one we could borrow for an evening?"

"You think he'd lend a car to just anyone?"

"I'm not 'just anyone.' Tell him we need it to save the world from evil villains," Ruby added.

Charlie shot a glance at Oliver.

"Close to the truth," Oliver said.

"Let me call him. He's probably got something in that old garage, but I haven't seen the guy drive in ages."

After a brief conversation on the corded phone at the corner of the bar, Charlie turned to Ruby and Oliver. "He'll be out back in a few minutes. I'll take you there." He gestured for the two to join him behind the bar. "This is the fastest way to the courtyard."

Charlie pulled open a hatch in the wooden floor, revealing a flimsy set of stairs leading to a dirt-floored cellar below. As Oliver placed his foot on the first rickety step, he was reminded of the cellar below the clockmaker's shop in Briarwood. Old wine racks lined the walls, and several large kegs sat in the corner.

"We roll the kegs right through the bulkhead door in the back," Charlie said, leading them through a low hallway to a storm door at the other end. "Easiest way to get 'em into the building." Charlie pushed the door open and shielded his eyes from the daylight.

An old three-car garage sat in a courtyard at the far end of the alley. The alley itself cut behind the back of a row of shotgun buildings and onto the street.

As they approached, rustling came from inside one of the open garage doors. Metal clinked and clanked as a man pulled a pile of parts from atop the hood of a tarp-covered vehicle.

"How's it hangin', Marv?" Charlie shouted.

The slender man turned toward them, holding the tail end of an old muffler.

"*The* Marv?" Oliver asked.

"Don't be fooled by what he's wearing. The man owns the entire block," Ruby replied.

"Perfect timing," Marv said. "Been cleaning out this old garage for the last week. Think I finally cleared away enough junk to pull *her* out." He slapped the tarp.

Marv hardly looked like a real-estate mogul, with grease smeared on his face and a ripped plaid cotton shirt.

With a dramatic flourish, he pulled back the blue tarp, revealing the olive-green hood of an old van underneath.

Marv lifted the hood, which protested with a loud squeak, and leaned over it. "Just had her out for a spin around the block a few months ago. Should be in relatively road-ready shape."

"Months?" Oliver asked.

After several minutes of fiddling under the hood, Marv stepped back to admire his work. "Let's try her out." He disappeared into the sliver of space between the van and one wall of the garage and squeezed into the driver's seat.

The engine struggled at first, sending a plume of black smoke drifting into the atmosphere, but after a bit of finagling, Marv got it to turn over, and the vehicle squealed to life.

The van slowly emerged from the garage as Marv carefully avoided clipping the side mirrors on the garage door's frame. The vehicle was a hodgepodge of parts—an automotive Frankenstein's monster with a poorly drawn sun spray-painted on its side, and the tailpipe continued to sputter black soot. Oliver thought Marv was playing a practical joke when he pulled the van from the garage.

"She's a beaut, isn't she?" Marv asked.

"She's *something*," Oliver replied.

"Keep her as long as you like," Marv said as he stepped out of the van, "but just try to return her in one piece. She's got sentimental value." He patted the van on the hood. "Had loads of fun with her when I was a teenager."

Oliver reached for the driver's side door, but Ruby stepped in front of him.

"I thought I'd drive."

"You drive?" he asked.

"I used to. I assume little has changed."

The passenger door was rusted shut, but Oliver pried it open with a few stern yanks.

"You've got to be kidding," he said once they were inside and safely out of earshot of the owner. "They'll see us coming from a mile away."

"We can't exactly pop in on the train, can we?" Ruby shot back, waving to Marv as they pulled through the alley. "If you have a better idea or another car, I'd be happy to let you take the lead."

Oliver looked down at his lap.

"I thought so," Ruby said. "I knew I should have bought that hearse when I had the chance. Caleb said it would have been good for lugging things around and promoting The Parlor. I didn't want to spend the money."

"You think a hearse is any less conspicuous than what we're in now?"

"I think you forget who you're working with," Ruby said. "We could drive into Christchurch in a tank, and they still wouldn't see us coming."

Gripping the steering wheel, Ruby drove down the alley and onto the street, running over the steep edge of the curb as she missed the driveway ramp.

"Not a word," she said as Oliver opened his mouth to speak.

"I was just going to offer to drive again," he said.

"It may have been a few years, but I'm still perfectly capable of—"

"Stop sign!" Oliver shouted.

Ruby slammed on the brakes as another car pulled through the intersection.

"Yeah, maybe you drive," she said.

The setting sun flickered between the trees as Oliver navigated the van around the twisty roads toward Christchurch.

The ride over was sickly quiet. Oliver had no clue what they would find when they arrived but hoped no one had been harmed. Asher would do no good to anyone dead, but Izzy hadn't heard the music and hadn't been affected by its powers. Surely there were others, like Martin. *What will happen to them?* His stomach churned as he considered the possibilities. But the Siren needed numbers, he assumed.

"What's our game plan?" he asked as he saw the Christchurch sign in the distance.

"Just surveillance for now. I need to see the lay of the land, then we can create a plan of attack. I'm sure we'd be able to pull a few recruits from the Unnatural Bar if need be."

Oliver expected to see a perimeter of townspeople guarding Christchurch and almost thought someone might have pulled the historic cannon from the entryway of the town hall and aimed it in their direction. To Oliver's surprise, the road to town was unguarded. Then again, a single wayward traveler would be no match for an entire town of hypnotized crazies.

He pulled the car to the side of the train station, just out of reach of the light from the streetlamps, and cut the engine. "If they didn't hear us coming from a mile away, I'd be shocked," he said. "This beast is loud."

"I've been keeping it under control," Ruby replied.

He rolled down the window to listen. The station was vacant and eerily quiet as the wind whistled through it. Aside from the breeze and the sound of the engine settling, the place was silent.

"I think it's safe," he said. "Let's get out and poke around."

They were careful to close the van's doors quietly and edged their way through the station to the entrance into Christchurch. The platform was empty, much as Oliver had left it the previous evening.

"You'd think we would have seen someone by now," Ruby whispered.

The shops around the town square were dark, except for the town hall, which beamed brightly in the distance. Instead of crossing through the center, by the founder's statue, where they would have been easily spotted, Oliver and Ruby edged around the periphery, by Fletcher Antiquities and along the outer wall of the hall.

The commotion from the hall floated out the windows and onto the streets. Although Oliver and Ruby were approaching in the shadows, the entire town seemed to be inside, leaving little reason to sneak.

Oliver pressed himself against the wall underneath a window and poked his head up to see in. The last time he did something like this, an angry guard had chased him through the briars, but no one was standing guard this time. Christchurch townsfolk filled the rows of seats, and he spotted Asher at the front of the room at the council table, hands tied to the chair with ropes. His concern-stricken face told Oliver he was still free of the Siren's spell.

Oliver scanned the crowd, and although most were sitting like obedient statues, a few others in the front row were tied to their chairs. The back of Izzy's head bobbed up and down as she struggled to loosen the rope.

Anna sat on the other side of the room next to Madeline and the other Elders, who apparently gravitated toward each other even under a hypnotic trance. Bev was nowhere to be found, though.

"Mom's missing," he whispered down to Ruby.

"Big surprise," she replied.

The Siren emerged from the doorway at the back of the hall and crossed the stage toward her violin. Something about her appearance seemed to put the crowd on edge. Many appeared exhausted, with deep bags under their red-tinged eyes. Anna was visibly shaking and looked ten times worse than when he'd seen her the night of Bev's attack.

The Siren seemed uneasy, too, as she looked out over the crowd. Her painted appearance had somewhat faded since Oliver had last seen her.

Oliver crouched back down behind the window.

"This is our chance. We won't have another opportunity like this," Oliver said. "Almost everyone is in one place, and we have to take advantage before she plays."

"I'm all for spontaneity, but shouldn't we get help? It's just the two of us against the entire town," she replied.

"Asher and the people in the front row are bound. She must not have played for them yet. If we can free them before she plays, they might be able to help. It's going to be a lot easier saving Asher if he wants to be saved. And once the town scatters, we may not have another chance to hit everyone at once."

"Are you sure about this?" she asked. "If something goes wrong, we've got no backup plan."

"We're fools if we don't take the opportunity," Oliver replied.

Ruby looked down, apparently sketching out a plan of attack in her head. "I'll give them enough of a scare to pull them out of whatever trance the Siren has them in."

"And while they're preoccupied, I'll grab the violin and smash it. We can't risk getting caught up in her spell too. And if anything goes wrong, we meet back by the van."

"Once it starts, you should be able to waltz right up to the front of the room. Just close your eyes if you get disoriented."

As the Siren tuned her violin, a shout came from the crowd. "Play!"

She ignored the call and continued to fiddle with her violin strings.

"We've done all you've asked. Now, play something!" Madeline stood up amidst the gaggle of Elders, shaking and agitated.

Oliver had seen her mad before, but this was different. She was desperate, starving for the sound of the Siren's violin. Oliver had assumed the people of Christchurch were hypnotized, but their cravings reminded him more of drug addicts searching for their next fix and having symptoms of withdrawal.

"We have a special guest tonight. This guest also

owes me payment before I put on another show for you," the Siren said.

Another voice came from the crowd. "We've waited long enough. Now, play!"

"We held up our end of the bargain. Play!" said another.

The audience chanted, "Play, play, play," and by the third refrain, all were on their feet.

"She's losing control of the crowd," Oliver said.

Ruby put a hand on Oliver's shoulder. "I think it's time. If we wait any longer, things might get out of control. Are you ready?"

"Ready as I'll ever be," he replied.

Ruby shifted her eyes toward the townspeople.

The commotion had already risen to chaotic levels, so the subtle shift in the ground was unnoticeable at first. The stone floor shook, seemingly rumbling from the anger of the mob. The townsfolk focused their rage on the Siren, who stood at the front of the room, preparing to play her violin. But as the shaking grew stronger, cracks raced across the floor, drawing the attention of the crowd.

Oliver quietly opened the front door of the hall and looked over at Ruby, who poked her head above the windowsill. She had started to shake. The feat would surely wipe her out, so he had to act quickly.

The cracks had become fissures, and the crowd

noticed the earth trembling under their feet. Before he could begin the perilous walk to the front of the room, the mob came rushing toward him, attempting to flee the building. He stepped toward one side of the room to allow them to pass, but the front doors slammed shut before anyone could escape into the square. The thought of being locked in an enclosed space with a crowd of crazed, hallucinating townies was almost too much to bear, but he swallowed hard and edged along the wall toward the front of the room.

As the crowd gathered at the front door, the earth opened, swallowing those not fortunate enough to step out of the way in time. A large chasm in the floor had obstructed Oliver's path toward the front, where the Siren stood frozen in fear and Asher sat confined in his chair.

It's an illusion, he told himself repeatedly.

He shut his eyes as screams of terror surrounded him. With a deep breath, he leapt forward into the pit. When his sneakers met solid ground, he kept running until he bumped into the edge of the stage.

With a firm grip on the edge of the stage, Oliver cracked his right eye. The Siren lay screaming as the stage crumbled around her, face pressed into the floor and immobilized by the illusion. Her long dreadlocks lay in a heap next to her. She'd been wearing a wig that had come loose in the chaos. Odd patches of gray hair covered her balding scalp. *She is an illusion too.*

The violin lay beside her, and Oliver reached for it, grabbed its weathered neck, then closed his eyes again.

The shaking halted as he raised the instrument over his head, preparing to smash it on the ground. He turned toward the crowd, many of whom had been completely incapacitated, bawling on the floor like upset children, pressed against the locked exit. Several even convulsed uncontrollably. However, the shifting ground had returned to normal, and the cracks had disappeared. He looked over at Ruby's window, but she was nowhere to be seen.

"Wait!" The Siren pleaded next to him. She scrambled to reaffix the wig to the top of her head. Scars and blemishes streaked her porcelain face where her makeup had smudged. "You can't. You don't understand what you're doing. They need the music. They need me."

Oliver looked at the crowd. They lay huddled in piles of tangled limbs scattered among the overturned furniture except for the few still bound at the front of the room.

"They don't need you anymore," Oliver said, hoping what he said was true.

He approached the front row of captives and loosened the ropes around Izzy's wrists with his free hand. "Are you all right?"

"Just cut me loose before they wake up," she said. Once freed, Izzy helped the others.

"I'm not talking about these fools!" the Siren shouted, flinging a hand toward the townspeople. "You don't understand, do you?"

"What are you talking about?" Oliver turned toward her.

"Do you think Simon could have arranged this from beyond the grave?"

Simon. This was solid affirmation that the man was involved.

"He thought Simon was a kook, that he wanted attention," she said.

"He?"

"People with nearly immeasurable power exist in this world, but no one can escape death. It's inevitable, or at least it was until he came along." She pointed at Asher, who was clinging tightly to his chair, still shaken by the imaginary earthquake. "He helped Simon carry out the plan, but he's expecting payment."

"And by payment, you mean—"

"Blood—eternal life—the only currency that matters now. Simon kept the boy hidden away in that little town, but now the secret's out. Unnaturals might do amazing things, but we're all bound by mortality, and Asher can change that. Those in power are eager to take advantage of his gifts. In exchange for a second chance at life, Simon had to make promises to share the bounty. Why do you think I'm here? A lowly old street performer. It's my job to help find Asher and keep Simon honest."

"But you don't need him. You have this whole town under your control."

"To the contrary, I need him very much." She gingerly pulled one of her leather gloves loose from her fingers and slid it off her arm. A full sleeve of tattooed flames ran down her arm and up to her wrist, but spindly varicose veins distorted the image. "Control and power mean nothing if you're dead."

Somehow, Asher had loosened the ropes binding him to the chair, and he rubbed his wrists.

"Do you have the key?" Oliver asked him.

Asher reached into his shirt and pulled out the Briarwood coin.

"Go out the back and wait for me at the edge of the briars." Oliver pointed at the Siren. "If you see her, your father, or anyone else besides me or Izzy, cross over."

"But you saw the body. It isn't safe," Asher replied.

"They were long dead. You don't have to go far. Just stay right on the other side until they leave. Simon won't be able to get to you on the other side without the key."

"I can't leave—"

"Just go!" Oliver yelled.

As Asher left through the back door, the Siren rose to stop him.

"Stay right there," Oliver said, cocking the violin back and threatening to throw.

"Where is Simon now?" Oliver asked.

The Siren smirked and pointed toward the back of the room.

As the crowd slowly regained their bearings and moved toward the front door, something seemed to hold it closed from the other side, preventing the townspeople from escaping the hall. Finally, one door opened, revealing the tip of a revolver, which caused the crowd to edge backward.

"As luck would have it, he's just arrived," she said.

Simon wasn't the only form in the entryway, though. Eric stood on his left, brandishing the gun, and Bev stood firm at his right. Eric turned and laced a chain through the front doors' handles then locked it closed with a padlock.

The strings of the violin dug into Oliver's fingers as he tensed. He had only a few moments before whatever remained of Simon would stroll up the aisle and prevent him from smashing the violin. He lifted the violin above his head and smashed its body on the stone floor. The neck snapped free, hanging by only a tangle of strings. Oliver tossed the broken instrument at the Siren's feet.

The Siren's expression soured. "What have you done?"

"I guess we'll find out, won't we?" Oliver turned to face the entryway.

Years of watching zombies and monsters lurch across movie screens hadn't prepared Oliver for what crept down the carpeted aisle. Simon had hobbled midway down the aisle, and now that he was closer, Oliver could see how corpselike the man had become. He was still a man, but his features had shifted and sagged as if Oliver had been looking at him through Ruby's menagerie mirror.

His hips hung at a slant on a broken frame he kept propped up with his elaborate cane. Eric guided him down the aisle on one side, with Bev on the other.

Oliver wondered why Simon had chosen his mother out of all the people in the town since she was no taller than five feet and was hardly built like a body-guard. Then he remembered—she'd been the one who found Asher. *It's her prize.*

Simon's facial hair had come in unevenly, leaving odd patches of white on his sunken face. The paper-thin skin covering Simon's body appeared almost translucent, and Oliver swore he could see veins underneath, glowing like some odd aquarium creature.

The tank of Asher's blood might have brought him back from the dead, but the man was only a shell of his previous self. Oliver wondered whether the cost of resurrection was worth it. The blood hadn't healed him, just allowed him to regain a semblance of life, like the fish in the tanks. Asher must have been right—his blood must not have worked on the dead as it did the living, and based on Simon's appearance, Oliver wasn't sure why anyone would want to live in that state. Some bits appeared to have been left in the under-world. *And how long will it last without another dip in the blood pool?* Eventually, the fish bones stopped jiggling.

As Simon walked down the aisle, the crowd pressed itself more tightly against the walls as though magnetized, but they were unable to escape through the locked doors. Clearly, whatever spell the Siren had sprinkled over the townspeople was lifted by Ruby's illusion. Oliver no longer had to concern himself with battling the entire town—his odds had just gotten significantly better.

When Eric noticed the shattered violin at the front of the room, he raised his revolver in Oliver's direction. "You've taken it from us."

Oliver looked for an escape, but the Siren was

guarding the back door. He lifted his hands in the air and hoped for some sort of mercy.

"Shoot him, shoot him!" Bev yelled. The words hit Oliver hard in the chest.

As he teared up, he locked eyes with her. Her expression was one of anger—one he'd seen many times before, but never this severe.

Oliver muttered the only word he could think of, in a soft, desperate whisper: "Mom."

As Eric clicked the hammer back, she twitched slightly, and her expression shifted from one of anger to fear.

She heard me.

"Let's not be brash," Simon said, breaking the tension. "We're not quite done with him yet, and we can get the girl another violin." He placed his grizzled hand on Eric's and pushed the gun toward the floor. "And a bullet's too kind for how much he's mucked up our plans, don't you think?" His *s*'s came out slurred, as if he hadn't yet regained full control of his speech.

"You," Simon said with disgust, turning his attention to the Siren. "Where is the boy? Why isn't he here?"

"There's been a snag."

Simon curled his lip. "Clearly." He looked around the room. "Couldn't even count on you to whip this town of old buffoons into shape."

"I can't just play whenever I feel like it. Playing takes energy. You promised to pay me before I had to play again." She wiped some smeared makeup off her cheek. "See what this is doing? I need his blood. I'm owed his blood."

"You had the boy right in front of you. You could have taken it yourself!" Simon wheezed at the edge of the stage and started a coughing fit. "Don't just stand there. Help me," he sputtered. He teetered forward and backward for a moment, trying to regain his equilibrium, then stood up straight again.

"What do you need?" Eric asked.

"A chair, you imbecile," Simon hissed. "Help me to a goddamned chair!"

The Siren pulled another chair from a corner of the room, and Simon hobbled over to it and fell onto the cushion with a loud wet squish.

"Lungs not working like they used to?" Oliver asked.

Simon drew his slender sword from its cane holster. Oliver felt a twinge of phantom pain in his side, where Simon had dug the blade in the year before.

"We won't have much time, now you've freed the town." A smile at one corner of his mouth was all he could manage as the other side of his face hung limp.

His yellow teeth shone through his parted lips. "Where is the boy headed?"

"I don't know," Oliver lied.

Simon cocked his head. "Let's not forget who holds all the power at the moment," he said, rolling the sword handle over in his hands, letting the light from the overhead lights flash off the metal.

"To the station," Oliver said. "I told him to wait for me in Amberley."

"He's a liar." The Siren stood between them. "He told the boy to wait for him at the edge of the briar patch."

Simon thought for a moment.

"You must think I'm foolish, that my little stint with death somehow cost me a few brain cells. We're going to go for a walk down the hill."

"Are you sure, sir?" Eric asked.

Simon smacked him in a shin with the flat of his sword. "Of course I'm sure. Just needed to catch my breath," he said, pushing himself up from the chair.

As Eric pushed Oliver toward the back door, he looked back at the townspeople. Izzy walked toward him, but he held his hand out for her to stay.

The Siren started to follow.

"You stay and deal with your mess," Simon hissed.

"You owe me," she said, moving toward him. "It's because of me you have him."

Eric stepped between them.

"*Had* him," Simon said. "And I will pay you. In the meantime, I recommend you hop on over to the music shop and find yourself another violin, or Eric here is going to be mighty angry when we return. You've promised him a show."

CHAPTER FIFTEEN

The march to the edge of the woods was more of a hobble as Simon struggled to maintain a steady pace. He'd barred the town hall's rear door and left Bev behind with the Siren to ensure the rest of the townspeople stay put.

Simon's hip bones clicked with each step, and his shoulders crackled as his body shifted. Eric held Oliver from behind as Simon clumsily stuck his cane into the soft earth to keep himself steady.

When they reached the tree line, Simon shouted into the forest, "Come out, boy!"

An owl called back, but Asher remained silent.

Stay in Briarwood. Oliver silently pleaded for Asher to stay hidden. "Guess he's not here."

"That would be unfortunate for you," Simon replied, pulling out his sword. He approached Oliver, struggling without the cane to support him, and pressed himself close. As he lifted the sword to Oliver's neck, the man's fetid breath crept into his nostrils.

"Time to come out now! I know you're hiding." Simon shouted, his voice strained and raspy.

"You're wasting your time," Oliver said, somewhat shocked by his own bravado.

"Come on, boy. Don't want me to hurt your friend, do you?"

Simon grabbed Oliver under the chin and lifted his head, exposing his neck. "Come out now, or I swear I'll lop his head off!" he screamed.

Asher's face appeared through the invisible barrier like a disembodied head floating across the patch. The wall seemed to cling to him as he stepped through, the edges of his silhouette outlined in a rainbowlike glow and water-like ripples radiating through the air around him. The briars folded beneath his feet and cleared a path to the edge of the woods. Asher's face was pale, as if the sight of Simon had drained all the blood from his body.

A sickly grin spread across Simon's lips. "Son," he said, "so nice to see you again." He released Oliver and pushed him toward Eric.

Asher stopped midway through the patch. "Spare the act, Father. I know why you're here."

"Isn't it obvious?" Oliver asked.

Simon turned around and gave him a spiteful glance.

"Without you, he's got nothing. He'll wither and die."

"Shut up," Simon said.

Eric squeezed the back of Oliver's neck hard, causing him to wince.

"If you want me, let him go!" Asher shouted.

Eric continued holding tightly onto Oliver.

"Do it, or I'll cross the barrier, and you'll never see me again."

Simon nodded back at Eric, who loosened his grip.

"Remember how he treated you!" Oliver shouted with desperation in his voice. "He'll lock you away."

"Enough!" Simon spat.

"He'll just keep coming!" Asher shouted from across the patch. "Death can't stop him. He's nearly destroyed Christchurch, all because of me. I won't let him hurt you too!"

"We can stop him. We've brought the entire town back from the brink, and we can figure out a way to stop him."

"I told you to shut up!" Simon smacked Oliver in the shin with the broad side of his sword. "Another word, and I'll put another hole in your side!"

Asher crossed the rest of the patch and walked toward Simon.

"That's right, boy. Now come along," Simon said.

Oliver had lost the battle. He thought back to when he'd first met Asher, malnourished and bleeding from wounds inflicted on him by his father, having no knowledge of the outside world aside from what he'd found in books read under the dim light of a dungeon lantern. Oliver had been so hell-bent on saving Asher that he hadn't realized the man was now perfectly capable of saving himself if he wanted to.

As Asher stepped toward Simon, shouts came from over the hill, and flashlight beams appeared, shining on the grassy horizon.

Simon let out an angry grunt. "Now, how did they get out?" He stepped toward the briars and tugged Asher along, hand gripped tightly around his arm. "Fine. Come on, we'll wait in Briarwood."

Oliver still wondered what mystical force Simon was waiting for. Simon stepped into the briars, which parted under his feet.

Asher looked back at Oliver. "I'll be okay. Tell Ruby goodbye for me, and thank your family."

Eric followed, but as a rogue vine snagged his foot, he second-guessed himself. Bev stood at his side, occasionally throwing a worried glance at Oliver.

Oliver expected Simon and Asher to vanish, but Asher stopped midway through the patch before reaching the invisible barrier.

"Get moving," Simon said, yanking on Asher's arm, but his son's feet remained planted firmly on the ground. "I swear I will make your life even more miserable than it already is if you don't pick up your damned feet."

"You need me more than I need you," Asher stated calmly.

"What are you talking about? Come on!" Simon yanked on Asher's arm again, but instead of conceding, Asher ripped his hand away.

Simon spun and reached for Asher, but he had already taken several steps backward.

"You need me more than I need you," he said again.

Simon's expression changed from anger to fear. He attempted to step toward Asher, but the vines had already strapped his feet to the earth.

Asher pulled the chain from underneath his shirt and dangled the coin in front of Simon. "Should have taken this first."

In an act of desperation, Simon pulled the slender sword from his cane and slashed at the vines. At first, he made enough progress to free one of his feet, but new vines moved in more quickly than he could clear them.

"Get back here," he pleaded, still trying to sound in control. "I'll spare the town. If something happens, more will come searching for you, and they won't be as kind to Christchurch as I have been."

"Spare the town?" Asher scoffed. "You're not in a bargaining position."

Eric paced desperately at the edge of the briars, helpless as the vines climbed up Simon's legs, tensing and ripping the fabric of his pants as they did.

The patch around Simon bloomed with bright-red roses as the vines pulled him toward the ground. The red flowers radiated outward until delicate roses covered the entire patch. The image brought back memories of the Witch, who'd fought against the same briars. The man let out a terrified scream as the brambles covered the rest of his body and wrapped around his face.

Just as the queasiness in Oliver's stomach subsided, the patch changed. The blood-red petals wilted around the edges. Eventually, the flowers dried, shriveled, and shed from the branches like dark-brown potpourri fluttering to the ground.

The sickness spread to the branches, and the deep-green brambles curled and snapped as if being set ablaze.

By the time Asher reached the edge of the patch, the briars had crumbled around him.

Something in Simon had poisoned the patch. Asher's blood had brought him back, but just like the animals confined to the tanks, he was different—tainted somehow.

Oliver looked toward the area where Simon's body had fallen and hoped to whatever beings were watching over him that the man wouldn't rise again. Eventually, the area cleared enough to reveal a glimpse of Simon's body.

Asher looked back in disbelief before turning to Oliver. "Didn't think it would be that easy," he said. "Wasn't sure the briars would want him."

"Does this mean there won't be any more music?" Eric asked, as though learning someone had canceled his childhood birthday party.

Oliver turned to face the remnants of Simon's shrinking army. Eric was standing with gun drawn and pointed at him.

"You've ruined it. You've ruined everything!" Eric screamed. He clicked the hammer back as Oliver looked for a place to run. Eric put his finger on the trigger, but before he could squeeze, he was distracted by a shout from behind as the two other Christchurch police officers approached from the edge of the field.

"Eric!" one of the officers shouted.

As Eric spun around, gun drawn, Oliver saw his moment and charged, plowing into him and knocking him down.

The officers seemed to be caught off guard by the

sudden show of violence and rushed in to help Oliver pin both of Eric's arms to the ground until he could pry the man's fingers from the grip.

Oliver tossed the gun aside. "Take it," he told Asher, who picked it up and pointed it at Eric.

"I want to hear it again. Let me hear the music again!" Eric screamed.

"Take him back up the hill—I'll be right behind you," Oliver said to the officers.

"Where's the other man?" one officer asked.

Oliver pointed at the briar patch and the exsanguinated lump in the middle. "He won't be going anywhere anytime soon."

As the officers turned toward the town hall with Eric, Oliver and Asher stepped into the patch of broken brambles. The patch crackled around him, the white noise of snapping limbs filling the night air. As the branches crumbled under their feet, Oliver reached a hand out to prevent himself from running into the invisible barrier.

The surface of the barrier felt like cool glass under his fingertips, but the surface was oddly uneven, almost rough. He could see the faintest trail of color following his fingers as they traced the glass.

Magic left behind. Ruby had said it the day they'd left to see Madam Marie.

Oliver had never thought of Ruby's or Asher's abilities as magic. Magic had always been clean and innocent —something he read about in childhood fairy tales. Even those who used their powers for evil—witches casting sleep spells and warlocks shrinking prisoners and holding them in teacups—seemed tame by comparison. But unnatural magic was real, grim powers bound in blood and bone that took a toll on those who used them. This magic was rough, like the surface of the dome, and covered in thorns, like the briars crumbling under his feet.

He stepped back and imagined how tall the invisible barrier must be. If someone had left this much magic behind, little must have remained in the caster.

Next to him stood Asher, his eyes glistening in the moonlight.

"Are you all right?" Oliver asked.

The question seemed to catch Asher off guard.

"I..." he started, but his voice wavered.

Oliver put his hand on Asher's shoulder.

"I killed my father," Asher replied. He looked down at his feet, surrounded by crumbled branches.

"He was already dead."

Asher hesitated. "Do you think what he said is true, about more people coming to take me?"

"He had to have help—the man was a prisoner. He couldn't have planned the entire thing from inside a jail cell nor as a corpse. But if more come, we'll face them together."

After a moment of silence, Oliver continued, "Come on. Let's go back. I'm sure they're worried about us."

They turned and made their way out of the patch and across the field. As he reached the base of the hill, a loud snapping caught Oliver's attention. He thought it sounded like a large branch breaking free from one of the forest oaks, but he turned to find a crack in the invisible Briarwood shield.

The break formed at the base, where the patch had consumed Simon, and stretched upward to Oliver's height. They waited a moment, but the rest of the dome seemed to hold steady for the time being.

As they reached the back of the hall, Oliver noticed the bar on the back door had been removed, which must have allowed the officers to escape.

"Go check on Ruby," Oliver said as he approached the back door.

Asher disappeared around the side of the building.

He expected chaos when he opened the door to the hall, but the townsfolk had already picked up the chairs and rearranged them into neat rows. Madeline was standing at the front of the room, conducting the ebb and flow of townsfolk passing through the hall.

The commotion stopped once the townsfolk noticed Oliver and Asher standing in the doorway.

"He's gone," Oliver said. "Dead."

Madeline strolled to the front of the room. "Thank God." She opened her arms for a hug but then seemed not quite comfortable enough to do so, so she patted him on a shoulder. Her eyes were tired, her face freed from its typical makeup mask.

Others gathered around them, townsfolk still woozy from whatever mystical force had held them captive for several days.

"Oliver!" Izzy parted the crowd, with Anna close behind, and squeezed him as hard as her arthritic grip would allow. "One officer went to radio the police in Amberley."

"To tell them what, exactly? 'A violinist has hypnotized the entire town, and a reanimated corpse is trying to kidnap his own son?'" Oliver asked.

She raised her eyebrows. "Well, when you say it that way..."

He turned to Anna, her eyes red and tears streaming.

"I'm so sorry," she said as he reached out for a hug.

"It's okay—really," he replied.

Although Izzy's hug had been dainty, Anna nearly crushed him with her muscular baker's forearms.

"Simon was just the tip of the iceberg. The Siren

mentioned someone else has been pulling the strings," Oliver continued. He looked around the room. "Speaking of, who opened the back door, and where'd the Siren go?"

Izzy pointed toward the far end of the room.

Bev stood near the rear of the town hall, wringing her hands next to Eric, who had been tied to a wooden chair.

"I'll be back," he said, leaving Izzy to comfort Anna.

Oliver approached, but Bev lowered her head and stared at the floor.

"Are you okay?" he asked, placing a hand on her shoulder.

She looked up at him but immediately jerked her head back toward the ground. "I can't... I can't look at you. I'm so embarrassed. I can't believe how I've treated you."

"You couldn't control yourself. No one in the town could."

"I nearly lost you today," she added, tears streaming. "I almost had a hand in killing you. I'm so sorry. I felt as if I was watching a movie, seeing myself act with no ability to control it. When Eric pulled the gun, something in me clicked, but I had to wait for the right time. When that evil man left me with the violin player, I saw my chance. As soon as I pulled the bar from the door, she took off."

The back door creaked open once again, and Asher and Ruby appeared in the doorway. As he turned toward the back door, Bev grabbed him by an arm.

"You saved the town," she said.

"No, we all did," he replied.

His mom grinned. "I'm proud of the person you've become. I love you, Son." She pulled him into a hug.

At first, the moment felt awkward and foreign, but as he wrapped his arms around his mom, his body relaxed. For a moment, the chaos and confusion of the night faded into the background, as if the two of them were the only ones in the room.

CHAPTER SIXTEEN

The sun rose as Oliver pulled the van into Amberley. He parked in front of The Parlor and exhaled as he cut the engine. Izzy and Anna pulled up behind him in the station wagon, ready to take him home, leaving Ruby to return Marv's precious van in one piece.

Ruby looked over at the building then stared down at her lap, seemingly unable to move her legs.

"Do you want us to come in for a minute?" Asher leaned in from the back seat.

"Just for a minute," she replied.

Oliver rounded the van and held the passenger door open for her. Her legs wobbled as he helped her step down to the sidewalk. Between the last night's illusion and the sucker punch Oliver assumed came from Eric, Ruby must have been exhausted. The sight of The Parlor couldn't have made things any easier.

She looked back at the van, hesitant to go inside. "Think I will miss our fair-weather friend. He's grown on me."

Asher put his hands on Ruby's shoulders and turned her toward the doorway of The Parlor. "We'll go in together," he said.

Oliver pulled back as Ruby and Asher stepped through the doorway and held up a finger to Anna and Izzy, still in the station wagon. Then he turned and stepped inside, remembering just how much damage had been done to the place.

"We can help you clean this up," he said. "You should have seen Izzy's house last year. We'll get it straightened out."

Ruby swallowed hard then strolled into the lounge with Asher and disappeared behind the bar.

"Thank God," she said, emerging with a bottle of absinthe and three glasses. "It survived." The bottle was the same special stuff Caleb had poured for Izzy and Oliver on the night Fred strolled up the aisle with a knife.

Without saying another word, she walked through the kitchen and out the back door to the courtyard, ignoring the surrounding chaos.

Oliver and Asher exchanged looks.

"Should we give her a minute?" Oliver asked.

"Are you coming, or do I have to drink this all by myself?" Ruby shouted through the back door.

She sat cross-legged in front of a patch of disturbed earth in the back courtyard. Oliver and Asher crouched next to her, and for a moment, all sat in contemplative silence. Oliver had no reason to ask what lay buried in the pit. He knew the answer.

Ruby set the glasses in front of them and filled them with the pear-colored liquid, not bothering to dilute it with water.

She downed the drink in a single gulp and poured a splash over the dirt.

Asher stared at the dirt patch. "I'm sorry, Ruby. I didn't know what else to do."

"Don't be dense," she replied, a slight edge to her voice. "You did what you had to do, and he likely would have killed me if you hadn't stopped him. Dead is dead, no matter how you get there, so we're just going to have to learn to live with it."

"I'm sure Asher can help you get the show running again," Oliver chimed in.

"I don't want him to come back here," she said. She looked at Asher square in the eye. "You should stay in Christchurch. It's for your own good." She punched the words like keys on a typewriter.

Asher's eyes widened. "But what about the show? Aren't you going to bring back the Menagerie?"

"The show's over. It was just as much Caleb's show as anyone else's. It doesn't feel right, going on without him."

"But what about The Parlor? You'll need help to keep it afloat."

"The Parlor can sit and rot, for all I care."

"What?"

"I'm leaving, Asher. I can't go on living here, sleeping in the bed where my husband slept and walking through the hallway where his body lay, pretending that nothing happened. I'm packing a bag and hitting the road for a while. I need to clear my head."

"Hitting the road? But this is your home. You love this place, and you and Caleb worked so hard to build it back up from nothing." Asher voice grew hoarse. "You can't just leave."

"Without Caleb, this place is just a pile of old wood." She shifted her eyes back to the dirt.

"But what about me?" Asher asked. "If what the Siren said is true, there'll be others looking for me. They know where to find me, whether I stay in Amberley or Christchurch. The only way to stay safe is to leave town. Let me come with you."

The last sentence caught Oliver by surprise. Asher

had been so timid about the outside world, but those fears seemed to have faded.

"We've got the whole town on our side," Oliver replied. "If anyone comes, you won't have to fight them alone."

Asher ignored Oliver and kept his eyes locked onto Ruby's.

"This is something I need to do on my own," she replied. "Stay in Christchurch and enjoy what time you have."

Asher shook his head and seemed angry at first, but his expression softened.

After they sat in silence for several minutes, she said, "I better get packing."

"Promise me you'll keep in touch, at least. You've got our number," Asher said. "That is, if Izzy lets me stay for now." He looked at Oliver.

"Is there any doubt?" Oliver asked. "At least check in every once in a while so we know you're all right."

"I will," Ruby replied.

They rose from the makeshift grave and headed through the house to the front door, standing awkwardly for a moment or two, unsure of how to say goodbye.

"Thanks for letting me be a part of your family," Asher said as he hugged her goodbye.

"You'll always be a part of my family. That won't change," she said. She looked at Oliver. "You too."

As Ruby shut the door behind them, Asher stepped back and took one last look at the large row house. "I will miss this," he said.

"We can still come back here," Oliver said. "Amberley is easy to get to."

"It won't be the same, though, not without Ruby and Caleb."

"Come on. Let's go home," Oliver said as he turned toward the station wagon.

CHRISTCHURCH WAS quiet for several days as the townspeople recovered from their collective musical hangover. The Siren had been right when she'd said the townspeople needed her music. Although the spell had been broken, those who had been affected seemed to suffer a withdrawal of sorts. Bev lay in her room for several days, and although Anna tried to tough it out and return to work, she, too, had to take a few days to rest.

Eric was the last in the town to be freed from the Siren's spell, but an hour alone with Ruby in Izzy's studio broke the subconscious hold. Oliver wasn't sure

what Ruby had done to the man—she wouldn't tell—
but he imagined it had something to do with the caricatures in Izzy's paintings.

Unlike the past year's events, what had unfolded
over the last few days was too big to ignore. The Siren
had hypnotized an entire town, and those lucky
enough to avoid the spell were chained together in the
town hall by their own families.

But the question of what to do about the situation
remained. Simon had been dispatched, and the Siren
had fled. If some shadow organization was looking
down upon them, who would believe them, and how
could they defend themselves against it? Regardless,
the townspeople seemed to agree on two key issues:
Asher was now a part of Christchurch and was
welcome to stay, and the people in the town would
stick together, no matter what creepy-crawly thing slid
past the town's borders to claim him.

Oliver's mom carried her own suitcase to the train
station this time around.

"You know, you can stay as long as you'd like,"
Oliver said.

"I couldn't possibly. I have a ton of things to do.
I've got to get back for a fundraising board meeting,
and I may even try painting," she replied with a smirk.
"You've inspired me."

"Well, you're welcome back anytime," he added.

"Think I've imposed on you enough for now." She let go of her bag as the train sat waiting in the station.

The two faced each other for an awkward moment, each searching for the right thing to say.

"I'm very proud of you," she said as she squeezed him hard. "Promise me you'll call now and then and maybe even come for a visit sometime soon."

"I think I could arrange that."

She climbed aboard the train, and he watched as she walked down the aisle to find her seat. He remembered the sense of dread he'd felt when she stepped off the train for the first time.

She was still Bev—too blunt and somewhat sharp around the edges—but during the past few days at Izzy's, she'd been markedly different. He hoped that this would be the beginning of a new chapter in their relationship—that they would have a relationship at all —and that her adventure with the Siren had given them common ground to stand on for the first time in his life.

Oliver strolled back to Izzy's, taking in the sights and sounds of Christchurch's square. The townsfolk had finally emerged from their homes and returned to business as usual.

As he reached Izzy's house, he heard a conversation coming from the back deck. When he rounded the house, Anna was sitting wrapped in a blanket at the back table with Izzy and Asher.

"I didn't know you were stopping by," Oliver told Anna.

"Izzy invited me over for dinner," she replied.

"Speaking of... Time to check the chili." Izzy looked at Asher. "Why don't you come give me a hand?"

As the two of them went into the kitchen, Oliver took a seat next to Anna. "Good to see you! How are you feeling?"

"Much better today," she replied with a smile. "How'd the goodbyes go with Bev?"

"Unusually pleasant," Oliver replied. "It's amazing what a blood-drinking zombie and an evil siren will do for a strained mother-son relationship."

"Glad to hear it." She laughed. "I'm still so mad at myself."

"Mad? For what?"

"For not being strong enough to resist the Siren," she said.

"No one in the town could. You couldn't help it."

"I know, but between you, me, Izzy, and Asher, I was the only one dumb enough to fall into the trap. I should have been there for you guys, and instead I helped her."

Oliver leaned in. "Don't tell Mom, but the only reason I wasn't chanting 'play, play, play' along with you was because she called me a sissy. Had I not stormed out, I would have been a drone with the rest of Christchurch. Being strong had nothing to do with it."

Anna looked down at the table. "Well, I'm sorry all the same."

"You can make it up with another night out on the town in Amberley," he replied.

"You've got a deal as long as we avoid any undead animal circuses, tarot cards, or psychic readings of any kind."

"Done."

Izzy and Asher emerged from the kitchen with a set of bowls and a heavy stockpot of chili.

"Dinner is served," Izzy said.

As they dug into the steaming bowls of chili, and Oliver instantly seared his taste buds, Izzy pointed her spoon in Asher's direction.

"You know, now Bev is gone, we could move you off of the floor and into the room across the hall," she said.

Asher looked up from his bowl, but before he could speak, a loud boom echoed from the forest in the distance.

The four of them stood and looked out toward the woods.

"It's breaking," Asher said.

Oliver shielded his eyes from the dusk sun, which sat just beyond the trees. The briars had never recovered after taking Simon, and whatever poison ran through his veins had slowly trickled up the large crack in the invisible barrier and splintered outward, forming a patchwork of putrid green spiderwebs. Pieces fell, much as they had done when the Witch put a temporary hole in the barrier a little over a year before, and as the dome finally shattered, sending a shower of glittering pieces down onto the hidden town, it didn't repair itself. They stood and waited, but the steady smoke Oliver had glimpsed when Asher grabbed his hand poured over the tops of the trees and into the clear sky. The edges of Briarwood lay in plain sight.

"What do you think they'll do when they realize the wall is broken?" Asher asked.

"Simon trained them to avoid the briars for centuries. I suppose that level of brainwashing can't be undone in a day—if anyone's still alive to notice," Oliver replied.

"They'll be able to see Izzy's house now—the beehives. Don't you think it'll pique their curiosity? If someone wants to cross, there's nothing stopping them."

For a moment, they all discussed the scenario, distracting themselves from the larger issue at hand.

Although they had rid the town of Simon once and for all, the invisible forces leading to his revival remained. Whoever was behind the plan to bring him back would surely show up on Christchurch's doorstep eventually, and they would be coming for blood.

ENJOY THE BOOK?

Continue the Journey with Book 3

Oliver Crum and the Blood Seekers

Check Out Chris Cooper's First Book

The Dreadful Objects

Please Consider Leaving a Review

Reviews help tremendously. Please consider leaving a review on Amazon or Goodreads!

Find an Error or Want to Keep in Touch?

Visit Dreadfulmedia.com to join our mailing list or report errors.

ABOUT THE AUTHOR

Chris Cooper is a writer, college professor, novice coffee roaster, and recovering engineer. He lived and worked in Japan, where he developed an obscure obsession for fancy fountain pens and currently lives in Ohio with his partner and Australian Cattle Terrier. Both enjoy going for walks. Chris writes supernatural thrillers full of colorful three-dimensional characters, macabre adventures, and twisty turny plots.